PRAISE FOR EMILY SCHULTZ AND *HEAVEN IS SMALL*

Trillium Book Award Finalist

"A young writer dubbed promising for her first three books, Schultz now keeps that promise: *Heaven is Small* is confident, disturbing, and clever, reeling us along, prodding us to notice the lame trappings of what we call living. . . . Schultz's voice is stronger than ever, her storytelling tighter, and her writing still replete with those trademark ziplines, surprising little protons of description that vault the reader into Schultz's unique narrative universe."   — *Globe and Mail*

"*Heaven is Small* [is] a stunning, often surprising read with moments of such audacity that the reader is likely to gasp out loud. . . . Schultz is an impressive talent . . . creating something new, something unique. The result is bold and winning, the sort of novel that satisfies on every level while managing to leave the reader with an afterglow of questions and observations."   — *Vancouver Sun*

"Schultz has created a delightful cast of lost souls . . . *Heaven is Small* is a keen examination of life and the afterlife, brimming with intelligence and wit."   — *Quill & Quire*

"Emily Schultz is one of those forces of nature that propels a literary scene."   — *Toronto Star*

"*Heaven is Small* definitely hits the mark. . . . Hilarious . . . Sensational . . . Poignant . . . Fun and smart all around."   — *NOW Magazine*

HEAVEN IS SMALL

EMILY SCHULTZ

ANANSI

Copyright © 2009 Emily Schultz

Hardcover edition first published in 2009 by House of Anansi Press Inc.

This edition published in 2010 by
House of Anansi Press Inc.
110 Spadina Avenue, Suite 801
Toronto, ON, M5V 2K4
Tel. 416-363-4343
Fax 416-363-1017
www.anansi.ca

Distributed in Canada by
HarperCollins Canada Ltd.
1995 Markham Road
Scarborough, ON, M1B 5M8
Toll free tel. 1-800-387-0117

Distributed in the United States by
Publishers Group West
1700 Fourth Street
Berkeley, CA 94710
Toll free tel. 1-800-788-3123

All of the events and characters in this book are fictitious, and any resemblance to actual persons, living or dead, is purely coincidental.

House of Anansi Press is committed to protecting our natural environment. As part of our efforts, this book is printed on paper that contains 100% post-consumer recycled fibres, is acid-free, and is processed chlorine-free.

14 13 12 11 10   2 3 4 5 6

LIBRARY AND ARCHIVES CANADA CATALOGUING IN PUBLICATION

Schultz, Emily, 1974–
Heaven is small / Emily Schultz.

ISBN 978-0-88784-956-5

I. Title.

PS8587.C5474H42 2010   C813'.54   C2009-906301-8

Cover Design: Ingrid Paulson
Text design and typesetting: Sari Naworynski

Library of Congress Control Number: 2010924027

  Canada Council   Conseil des Arts   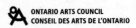 ONTARIO ARTS COUNCIL
for the Arts   du Canada   CONSEIL DES ARTS DE L'ONTARIO

We acknowledge for their financial support of our publishing program
the Canada Council for the Arts, the Ontario Arts Council,
and the Government of Canada through the Canada Book Fund.

Printed and bound in Canada

"If this is Heaven ah'm bailin out!"
— "Mutiny in Heaven,"
The Birthday Party

PART I

SEPTEMBER/OCTOBER

1

MOMENTS AFTER HIS DEATH, an event he had failed to notice, Gordon Small sought new employment.

Welcome to Heaven. If you know the extension you wish to reach, enter it now.

Gordon cradled the receiver and waited for further instructions. *For a company directory, press the star key. To return to the previous menu at any time, press pound.* He hit the asterisk, selected Human Resources from a long list of options. After a few minutes of fast, nervous talking, he had secured an interview.

To get to Heaven, Gordon took the subway, then another subway line, then a bus.

He was accustomed to walking to work. His previous job, as manager of Whoopsy's Gags 'N Gifts, was only two blocks from Mrs. Ashbridge's, where he had rented a room for the past seven years. His street was named after a potato — Russet Avenue. The neighbourhood where he lived was crowded with churches, but nonetheless plagued by scuffles in the subway, and even the odd shooting. One block over, on

Pauline, an immense brown-brick Catholic church huddled, surrounded by sumac trees. There was the Islamic mosque at the cross street, and right outside the subway the Baptist job with its sign of vinyl letters and constantly changing slogans. *Think spiritually, act righteously. Hell is Heaven's alternative lifestyle. For maximum pain relief, try forgiveness. Dusty bibles lead to dirty lives. All roads lead to hell, except one.*

In comparison to the mopped passageways of the mall, with its neon kiosks of Wireless Waves and Lotto, the subway was a dreamlike concept in a whole new set of hues, subdued and sickly. Gordon recalled the big L-shaped mall with its shiny tiles, its smell of coffee and Mr. Clean, its parade of continually changing fads. The clothing stores seemed to switch names every season. Each September recruited a new fleet of sixteen-year-old faces to gawk at Whoopsy's merchandise as if it had just been invented — rainbow Slinkys, punching nuns, mini disco balls, TV-sloganed T-shirts, fuzzy handcuffs. Soberly name-tagged, hair and patience thinning, Gordon had stood behind the counter for seven years, watching blush-brushed teens in low-cut jeans and lime green G-strings bend with laughter.

As manager, Gordon had never scheduled himself before ten. Even 11 a.m. was obscene. A bright university senior named Ricky had opened the store and handled things for the first hour or two; Ricky eventually begat Jane, a reliable young mom who preferred part-time, and Jane begat Andrew, and Andrew begat Yashin, and Yashin begat John, and John begat Claudia, and so on and so forth for seven years.

Now Gordon reflected that in some ways public transit, with its pale, caffeinated faces, was ruder than the boob-shaped ice

cubes and *Oh Lordy, Who's 40?* coffee mugs he had been peddling since his divorce from Chloe. There wasn't one person
on the subway who looked like somebody he would want to
know. First, everyone came dangerously near to jostling him
and no one glanced in his direction. He had to fight for space
just to wrap his hand around the pole. Second, everyone was
crunched into their clothes — black and charcoal, bile-thick
beige and flavourless-as-chalk blue. Everyone wore sensible
shoes. There were no urban cowgirls at this time of day, no
boys sauntering sweatshirted with their hoods and hand-
knocks. Everyone was pressed upright in their plastic seats,
creased inside their pants. From the Christie to Bay stops,
Gordon watched the ribbing of his dark socks beneath his
dark cuffs. From Rosedale to Summerhill, he memorized the
brush-scrubbed cuticles of his nails and ignored the sinewy
knee-backs of taupe women, pink women, mint-green. At
Davisville, like everyone else, he stared straight ahead. He
didn't think of incest or war, cheerleaders or wrestling, the
catastrophes of skin or human nature, the jailed semen in his
lower half anxiously awaiting release, the way that he had at
Whoopsy's, where the staff worked in environs of simulated
farts and oversized blow-up beer bottles. Gordon rattled his
way north, airless, lightless. The train began to move at double
speed, and Gordon could imagine fields and wildflowers
whirring over his head.

He avoided eye contact and memorized the answers per-
missible to give in any and every interview situation. He
pulled out a folded piece of paper with blue lines on it, torn
from a spiral notebook. In his tight scrawl:

- *The Heaven Book Company: largest purveyor of romance in the world*
- *14 dif. lines of romance titles (dif. markets/"imprints")*
- *owner of several print media corps, delivery companies, and affiliate of several perfumeries, undergarment plants, "frozen treat" companies, etc., etc.*
- *Higher annual income than Hallmark Cards*
- *Heaven's Sealed with a Kiss Club = books by subscription*
- *From Heaven FAQ … Regarding the number of Heaven releases in a single year, if all romance novels including translations were laid end to end, they would circle the globe 1.5 times.*
- *From Heaven FAQ … The average Heaven "bachelorette" reader will spend the same amount on Heaven titles as she does on one month's groceries. In comparison to her single male counterpart, she will admit to spending nearly twice as much as he does on his erotic materials/aids. "And why shouldn't she? Her heart has its secrets too."*

Gordon had taken down this last quote directly from the Heaven web site because it had struck him as particularly strange. He was not sure how Heaven had come by these statistics, yet he found he did not doubt them. So far as Gordon had been able to divine, Heaven was proud: love was winning out over cheap sex and sustenance. Or not love really, but desire for romance. Gordon thought about those words: *desire for* romance, not actual romance itself.

The train broke from the tunnel that had separated it from a nacreous sky. The tracks ground upward toward grass, and the grass waved the train on, letting Gordon and his co-travellers pass — the thousand or so of them in a capsule, hands clasped together, silent save for their hidden hearts. Gordon's chest constricted each time he thought of standing at the base of Heaven's stairs, of walking toward that building, closing in on his appointment.

He stretched his neck and looked up and down the car. They had lost some along the way. The woman with the bumpy, fist-sized knees had gone, taking her sculpted bronze hair with her. The Korean lady with the floral blouse and broad, padlocked face had disappeared too. The man who was constantly turning his wedding band seemed to have escaped with her. Now, positioned in a seat beside-yet-facing Gordon's was a fellow in a pinstriped suit, his eyes downcast in spite of the light pouring in all around them. The man's eyebrows were like dark tildes.

The train plunged underground again. A clatter of stops. A huff and puff of stop and go. A man across from Gordon held a Hindi newspaper on his lap, its letters shaking between fingers that folded and refolded its sections. He did not appear to be reading, simply rearranging. The whole ride, he and Gordon had stood and sat periodically, bound by an honour code to which no one else seemed to subscribe, judging who was worthy of their seats by the number of lines in their faces, the height of their shoes, or the weight of their bags. Gordon felt a kinship with him. They had stood together twice. Once for the pregnant business-coordinates blond, her belly like a second briefcase. She'd taken the other man's seat. Again they'd stood for the blind man who lacked a dog. Everyone else rode without looking beyond feet, newspapers, romance novels. Gordon had forgotten that people still read — well, dozed and read, read and dozed, shuffled and dozed, read and shuffled.

He now paid close attention to the women in the car with novels, looking to them for keys to what lay ahead of him. One actually held against her chest the much-thumbed pages of a throbbing Fabio and his maiden, red dress half undone, a wanton collarbone that seemed to split the cover in two. Gordon's eyes rode this reader's features. Her pupils never took in his gaze. She was dolphin-shaped, humped beneath her white shirt, jade jewellery mottling her throat and ears. Her hair formed a silver halo around her face. The questions Gordon wanted to ask her! Her, and all of his fellow travellers, sliding as they did, gracefully, awkwardly away. Each station led to other lives, from which he was forbidden.

As the train became more and more empty, it occurred to Gordon, not for the first time, how limited his life had become.

The train stopped abruptly inside the dark tunnel — making piercing rusted sounds, scraping, and then silence. The lights went out.

In the dark, Gordon brought his fingers up to his chest pocket. Beneath them, beneath his suit jacket, and beneath a layer of shirt pocket hovered a one-by-one-inch box, and inside it, the tiny white tablets that had become a kind of touchstone. Although Gordon took them only once daily, over the years he had developed a nervous habit of feeling for them to be sure they were still there, camped close to his chest. Before Gordon could begin to worry about missing his connection or being late for his interview, before the conductor's voice could come over the speaker, they were off again. The subway lights flickered to full blast, and those who were left blinked and laughed and said, "Oh!" The train harrumphed forward. Gordon wondered who it was who had died at that remote station, and how far down the tracks he had been yanked. No wonder no one made eye contact.

His regular routine had meant that he rarely travelled outside a thirty-minute radius. Over the years Gordon's friends had fallen away as they moved to more distant climates and began that most selfish of all things: the raising of children. They had emigrated. To a country of prams. Gordon had limited himself to confidants within the closest range. At night at the Brass Taps, a bucket of beer could be shared with Grenwald, the manager of Champs Sports, one of the longest-standing stores in the mall. Like Gordon, Grenwald was perpetually broken-hearted, a long-time girlfriend having left him three years back to pursue a career in acting out west. Unlike Gordon, Grenwald perpetually saw action. His banter on both topics — love and sex — was about as entertaining as a roast beef sandwich with Swiss. It filled the time, and the stomach, and then Gordon would exit, feeling warm, full. Go home to his adopted grandmother/landlady and the ball game.

Mrs. Ashbridge could barely climb the stairs, in fact had not since the day she had shown him the room for rent. Even then she had stood at the landing and gestured, puffing, one hand on the rail. "There's the bed, and the *divan*," he remembered she had called it. "The kitchen" — she'd pointed to the clothes dresser atop which a variety of three-pronged appliances sat. "The bath." It had come furnished, the bed and a blue settee dominating the room. The bed was an iron frame from 1945 and a mattress that had been replaced some time in the '70s or early '80s. To these items Gordon had added an oversized television, an old-fashioned typewriter whose ribbon always dried out before he could use it, and a bookshelf stacked with his motley finds. At night he would take a walk around the block to inhale sweet basil tokes — the instant tingling of a thing that, rolled in paper, brought another life to Gordon's life. In the mornings, when his mouth felt mashed with weeds, the Vivatex tablet would find its way into his palm and from there down the hatch, usually amid a mouthful of instant coffee. Inside him the medication emitted a time-released happiness. It felt like a pleasant but constant yawn.

Now Gordon tried to picture the unknown of Lillian Payne, the human resources director who would interview him today. Would she be blond or brunette?

He imagined Lillian Payne sitting beside him, replacing the wheezing businessman with the Lolita-like softness of a slip-knot. Her small white hands were tying themselves around each other like two silk scarves. Awaiting Gordon was a platoon of short-skirted women at desks, all wet behind the knees, and constantly wet between them from reading romance. The pinstriped man got off at Lawrence, and Gordon could feel himself surging ahead, sailing on, on, and on toward something more *something*, though he didn't know what.

DEPOSITED ABRUPTLY ON A GRIM platform where he was to catch his final bus, Gordon found himself alone.

He wished he smoked. He stood and stared off in the direction that he supposed the bus would come from — a patch of gummy wall turned in from the street to the half-covered station. Beyond it Gordon could see an oblong stretch of sky, less pearl than before, the rain having ceased sometime between downtown and the place he now inhabited. Gordon had left home over an hour before and, if he were lucky, would complete his dreadful journey within the next twenty minutes. It occurred to him that he did not really know where he was going. It could take five more minutes or five more years.

He gazed about the vacant station.

"Hello," he said aloud to himself.

The T shape of the station roof carried his voice across the platform, with no one but him to hear it. "My name is Gordon Small . . . I'm here for the interview. . . I'm here to see Ms. Payne. If you could just tell Lillian I'm here for — Human Resources, please. Lillian Payne. I'm thrilled to meet you. I've been looking forward to this interview because — Why would I like to work at Heaven?" Gordon's voice built. "What would we have without romance? Love is all around us; I think I understand that without having read as much of the genre as some. But really, it's spelling that matters." Gordon tried a finger in the air. "Deadlines. I am a great organizer. Detail-oriented. Perfectionism is my greatest fault. No. *Start again.*" Gordon's index finger dropped. He stared at the oil-stained cement where the bus would pull up, at the blank schedule mounted on the pillar to his left, at the vacant ticket booth.

"Hello," he said. His voice skidded across the concrete like some misused piece of rubber. *Louder.*

"Hello. My name is Gordon Small."

2

HEAVEN LOOMED. Gordon had just two minutes to spare as the final lurch of the bus ejected him onto the curb with lethal precision. In spite of the time, he paused, stared up. He couldn't help but consider the Egyptians. It had taken them more than twenty years to construct the Great Pyramid at Giza, the premises where their king would be buried. In comparison, the housing for Heaven Books was perhaps not a major accomplishment. But only if the two were compared scientifically, side by side. By pedestrian standards, Heaven was mighty. Its glass façade entered a cloud and mirrored back the sky. Though the day had been ducking its head in and out of fog, revealing a kind of twilit morning, the tower rose undeterred, defiantly sparkling. He couldn't understand why he'd never heard of it, why the building hadn't been named a national landmark. The Great Pyramid had been constructed by hand, but a lot of cranes had obviously been needed to build Heaven.

The building was surrounded by a moat of printing and packing houses, a cul-de-sac of one-level industrial plants.

Taking stock of the way he had come, Gordon noted that, besides Heaven, the bus route seemed to serve only a Good-2-Go cafeteria, a Print Three, a cardboard manufacturer called Box It in Seven Seconds, an outlet store for Nine West shoes (which Gordon imagined jammed with brown rows of odd-shaped leather toes under sullen fluorescents), and a desolate Motel 6.

As Gordon snapped to attention and passed the gold sign emblazoned with Heaven's company logo, he fixed his reflection with an equally gold, frightened grin. The company letters were carved two knuckles deep. In his reflected image Gordon's ears hugged either side of the lower basin of the *a*. Without further delay he ran up the concrete steps.

Inside the lobby a vacant-eyed security guard was posted behind a mirrored desk. The setting struck Gordon as resembling a little girl's jewellery box, and for a second he envisioned the guard turning in circles on one toe. Instead the man crossed his arms over his blue cotton chest. Gordon showed his ID and filled out a requisite form while the man called up HR's Lillian Payne on a telephone that didn't require any dialling. Then he leaned back, waiting. Gordon waited with him. They both stared at the elevator doors, watched the small bright numbers click down. She was travelling from the very top. Floor Seventy, Floor Sixty-Nine, Sixty-Eight, Sixty-Seven . . . The doors were silver against a brushed velvet wallpaper of pale pink. Floor Fifty-Two, Floor Fifty-One . . . A slim silver trash can stood at attention to the left. Floor Thirty-Three . . . The wall gave way to hallways on either side. A light-box hovered, jutting out about a foot above Gordon's head, on which the word WOMEN glowed, a white beacon in one alcove. In the other, MEN, dimmer, one of the bulbs burnt out. Floor Fourteen, Floor Twelve . . . The ceiling vaulted overhead in carved half-circles, art deco in plaster, mallish. A set of unclimbable steps. Floor Five, Floor Four, Three, Two . . .

The security guard cleared his throat.

Gordon smiled.

"Nice suit."

Gordon peered down at it, carefully considering each olive button. They were new. Each felt heavy as a roll of coins on his chest, though Gordon could not remember draining his bank account to pay for the ensemble. "Thanks."

The elevator doors slid open. Lillian Payne stepped out.

The shock of her red hair against the pink wallpaper lit a nervousness inside Gordon. Her face bore the pearl trans-parency of an embryonic sac. Her slate eyes were cut above razor cheekbones. She wore men's-style dress pants, black, and a red mandarin-collared jacket, one small silver clasp over her throat. "Mr. Small," she said, without a question mark in her voice. She had come to take him up. Her lips twitched into a dubious smile.

Gordon had not prepared for the awkward intimacy of the elevator ride. He could tell that Lillian Payne was one of those people who always acted quickly, and with aplomb, and expected the same of everyone else. Though attractive, she managed to exude *cruel* from every tight pore. The idea of being in a room alone with her — indeed, the small room of the elevator — frightened Gordon immensely. They shook hands, exchanging a static shock, at which Gordon cringingly mumbled, "Ow!" Even more cringingly, he found himself adding a sneeze of anxious laughter. Then, with no other options, they stepped inside the lift together. She was a good two to three inches taller than Gordon, at least six feet in height. Her short hair pitched at odd angles around her face: something styled by running one's hands through it, palms puttied with product. Gordon noticed that those hands were long, unwrinkled, as she reached to depress the Close button. The security guard stared after them blankly. As the doors shut out his ennui eyes, Gordon nodded goodbye.

Lillian swiped a yellow light with her plastic card. The control panel swatch turned to green and up they went, their backs to the mirror, elbows resting tentatively on a handrail. They stared straight ahead at a corrugated diamond pattern etched in the steel doors. Around the top, hidden tubing peed pristine light across the ceiling. Gordon wished he couldn't smell her (lemon and leather) and hoped she couldn't smell him (dampness and Altoids). She had a stringy, muscular body that looked as if the day she had been poured from the genetic vat she'd hung onto a bar while the rest of her body dripped down, icicle-like, and hardened: hips and legs as narrow as a splinter.

"Nervous?" She turned to face Gordon. Her eyes glinted with bemused appraisal.

"No," he lied. Gordon had never read an actual romance novel, and he was certain that this was a question he would not be able to tap dance around.

Though he had hoped to wow "Call Me Lillian" within the first thirty seconds of this journey, it was she whose eyes travelled up and down his sleeves and pant legs as easily as if scanning the weekend classifieds. When she reached Gordon's face, her eyes seemed to change colour. Her chin tilted. Nonchalant "Call Me Gord" broke the gaze and stared at Ms. Payne's shoes. They were oddly ordinary: flat, with black buckles, the top of her foot exposed, an egg-coloured nylon oval.

Swipe cards entered and exited, dangling on cords around necks and wrists. "Hello Sonja" got on at Floor Sixteen and rode to Floor Forty-Two with them. She had hair so thin and brown it looked like someone had grilled it onto her head. Her face had "Computer Wallpaper: Niece and Nephew Department Store Portrait Series" written all over it. Gordon could already see her dustless desk, a parade of Cracker Jack toys artfully arranged, and one of those totem collections so enjoyed by true individuals — frogs or fish, elephants or owls, anything that could be gathered obsessively in fuzzy denominations or painted onto wooden clocks and other craft items. She was twenty-eight at most and, Gordon felt, far too young for such tragedies. She bubbled with updates about foreign rights — "Just got the newest batch in from Japan. You should see how the covers look!"

Lillian answered this exclamation in a monotone: "*Konichiwa*, Heaven Osaka."

When Hello Sonja had departed, Lillian looked Gordon up and down again, exciting sweat cells in his forehead region, underarm regions, neck region, crotch region, and all other regions. The ride was rivalling his transit time.

"Policy states that the interview cannot begin until you're signed in with reception in HR. But it's a long way up," Lillian said. "Tell me about yourself — something legal, within bounds."

Gordon glanced at her.

She smiled genuinely, exposing crystalline teeth. "Don't make me pry."

"Small talk?"

"Yes, and absolutely unrelated to anything we have to discuss upstairs."

"Off the record?"

"Mm-hmm. Travel. Geography. Hobbies. Sports. Cooking. Dogs or small children . . ." She turned in to him, personal-like but not, flicking her wrist.

Dogs? Small children? Gordon stood there pondering, the rail behind him searing the first crease into his jacket. Was this part of the psychological testing? The woman actually blinked at him, the serration of her red eyelashes a prompt. Because she seemed to command it, he answered her in absolute order. "Paris once. North America, most of it. The Pacific Rim someday soon." The latter a lie, based on Hello Sonja's suggestion of the world of Heaven beyond Heaven Central. "Russet Avenue, just west of Dufferin. Baseball, sure. Soccer, take it or leave it. Eating more than cooking. Who doesn't like dogs and children?"

Lillian's lips quirked into a wry brown corner where a pale mole was telling some private joke to two pink freckles. "I think you'll fit in just fine here," she said, as if they were not about to step into the HR foyer, but out of it.

The Human Resources office was the hue of nipple meeting flesh. Lillian escorted him past a reception area into her own office, which was vast, housing what appeared to be an archive of every title published, neatly arranged by spine colour.

"This year's," Lillian said when Gordon asked.

Lillian explained that a Ms. Chandler Goods, the head of the Editorial Department — or "Ed. Head" — was overseas at present, otherwise Gordon would have had a group interview. Instead it would be just herself and the supervisor from Proofreading. The latter arrived on cue, looking as if he had dressed for a part in a film about a publishing company. He wore a brown vest and his sleeves were rolled up, as if he considered himself a hard worker. Before the questions began, Lillian and Jon — as Proofreading was called — batted enthusiasms back and forth about the Editorial Department at large, as if they seldom spoke and were taking this opportunity to make up for lost time while impressing their new recruit.

"Yes, yes, I've heard that Chandler Goods is a young international dynamo!" the supervisor exclaimed — oddly, Gordon thought, as if he couldn't wait to have someone above him. "When will we all meet her?"

"End of October. November, if there are problems with immigration."

"Worth the wait, Ms. Payne. Worth the wait, I'm sure."

Before Gordon could interrupt with small talk or questions of his own, Lillian whisked out two folders and handed one to Jon. She let Gordon know that if he were accepted, he would be registered with their temp agency, Job City — or had he already registered? — and technically would work under that umbrella for a brief period until he was approved for full-time. Then they ran through the questions quickly, as if an egg timer had been set.

How did you first hear of Heaven Books? What prompted you to apply for work in our Proofreading Department? What makes you think you would be an asset to our company? Why do you want to join Team Heaven? Is there anything else we should know?

Gordon stumbled over his motives for contacting Heaven, but the rest of the questions he answered with ease, almost as if he had been working up to them his whole life. There was a tense moment when the two Heaven representatives peered at him following the *Is there anything else . . .* query, and the question seemed to repeat itself in the space between them until Gordon shook his head fervently, *No.*

When Lillian and Gordon concluded the interview with a handshake, he felt the dry shock as their skin lit up painfully again. "It was nice meeting you, Mr. Small — Gord." Then the woman who held his future in a folder stuck one wrist quickly through the elevator doors and swiped Gordon into the lift's elaborate code. "You'll hear from me very soon." She smiled as the doors clasped one another, holding Gordon tight within.

Alone, he fell the seventy floors on a fluid hydraulic system that could barely be felt until it touched the earth.

3

THEIR THROBBING MALEHOODS were ball-less, only shafts, stitched on at the groin. It was as if the authors — the floral-printed Peggys, Marthas, and Marys — had carried out love affairs with marital aids. Gordon tossed *Virgin for Hire* onto the empty bench beside him and picked up *No Business Like Show Me Business*.

He sat at the bus stop outside the Heaven building for what seemed like weeks. In a studious after-interview stupor he turned pages that were peopled with flesh but not-flesh. Acts akin to pornography glided over dewy thatches, tender nubs, and downy notches, hard heats and rock-rigid sexes. Just reading the words made Gordon think creepy thoughts and duck his head.

The heroes came to climax with long moans. Multiple *H*'ed *ohhhhh*'s spanned the page, but there were never any secretions. Explosions abounded but mess did not. The heroine's hair was always charmingly mussed. Her nipples were teased into taut peaks before her lover had even touched them. If there were condoms (and the trend seemed occasional at best), they were frantically pulled on before the male "impaled her to the hilt." There was no removal, no threat of disease or unwanted pregnancy, no ungainly search for a trash can or a box of Kleenex. There was no need to bathe, save for the pre-third-date Calgon scene where the woman delighted in the suds and thought of her man.

And oh, what a man! A man who knew what he wanted: her. A man who was so damn smart. A man who would gaze at a woman's mouth before he kissed it. A man made of money, and height, and heat, and BMW smoothness. A man with dark, exotic eyes who smelled of the woods. A man of solid presence, moulded contours, and sloe-eyed glances, with big hands but sleek thighs. A man written by women. One who plunged and panted, grunted and growled, pounced and pawed playfully. Like a lustrous oversized cat.

Lillian Payne had bestowed all this upon him post-interview. "Perks," she'd called the stack of gleaming paperbacks. Did he want this job? Gordon asked himself. He stretched one arm over the grubby painted wood slats of the bench as he skimmed the cramped pages, characters jumping and trembling beneath his thumbs, still no bus in sight.

The female, as she was often called, fared no better than her partner. She was stubborn but frequently ditzy, in spite of her sophisticated career as a CEO, fashion designer, or magazine editor. If she had children (and the widow or divorcee did), she always put them ahead of her own needs. If she had a dark past (and even the most virginal had learned not to trust her instincts), she looked to her new suitor to solve it, simultaneously pushing his muscled chest away. If she had been taken captive (forced into marriage by some familial obligation or loophole in a will), she would fiestily fight her captor's straightforward rapes, admonishments, and cruel torments — only to give in to the torment of her own desire.

As clumsy as she was beautiful (five feet nine, with swollen, beckoning lips and tendrils of blond hair spiralling down at the most inopportune times), she spilled coffee on her soon-to-be boyfriend's shirt because of the delighted distraction of his stormy blue eyes. Alliteration, repetition, and an outdated earnestness were the cornerstones of the genre. Attraction was not only abundant but redundant: so honest, so deep, so fathomless. The male was devastatingly handsome and sinfully sexy when the female described him to herself in moments of submission. Eventually Gordon found himself dragged in by the predictability and cartoonish charm of the stories.

When she wasn't admonishing herself for "loving that man," the heroine abhorred him, competed with him, and was determined to prove herself smarter. In the end she gave in to her feminine instinct. She spent hundreds indulging herself *just this once* with extravagant underwear, and spent thousands on subterfuge. She hired friends or fellow models to attempt to turn his head or tease out his secret, since he could never *ever* possibly *really* care for *her*. (Gordon noted: *Italics take precedence over strong verbiage.*) She took cabs to New York galas, hid behind potted plants, engaged in lipstick slapstick. She was Nancy Drew with a perpetual nipple hard-on, headstrong, with a nine-year-old's smarts and a nineteen-year-old's desire. She was instantly naked, her hair constantly, gorgeously windblown. She was not looking for someone to complete her, but he had, seamlessly, done so as she dug her nails into his broad shoulders, in spite of herself. She could turn on her heel and switch tenses that quickly too. And, as she tilted her chin, nationalities. Her eyes were as turquoise as the American Southwest where she was born; her will was as cold as the Canadian North; her heart was as wild as the outback of Australia; her lips were as misty as London. She was looking for her cowboy, her Mountie, her game warden in the outback, her jet-setting businessman.

Of all the bad clichés, there was just one left out. The Gordon Small.

4

GOOD MORNING, GORDON.

You must be new. You must be Gordon. Hi, Gordon. Gordon? Oh, you're Gordon! I guess you're Gord. Gord! Good for you. Oh good, you're here. Into the glorious gadgetry of Heaven, Gordon glided, past gadolinium-haired girls, golden waving ones, and giggling, gossiping groups. A cappella *Gordon, Gordon, Gordon.* Gorgeous. A gap-toothed gamine gang singing in a chorus of G major . . .

Hi, I'm Amber, I'm Angel, I'm Anne-Marie, Becky, Bella, Bliss, Carma, Carolyn, Catherine, Daniella, Desreen, Donna-Sue, Edie, Emily, Erika, Fiona, Fleur, Francine, Gabrielle, Georgia, Georgianne, Helen, Hazel, Hilary, Ingrid, Iris, Ivy, Jessica, Judith, Julia, Katrina, Kennedy, Kylie, Lena, Lizette, Lucy, Marguerite, Marietta, Manjeet, Nancy, Naomi, Nathalie, Olive, Oona, Oxana, Patricia, Pauline, Petra, Rachel, Ray-Anne, Ruby, Sarah, Sally, Stella, Tanya, Tina, Toni, Ulrikka, Unta, Ursula, Vanessa, Veronica, Virginia, Xandra, Xaviera, Ximena, Yasmine, Yolanda, Yvonne, Zhang, Zora, Zsa Zsa.

For the first day or two, women swung in and out of Gordon's cubicle checking up on him, saying, "Don't worry,

Gord, you'll get the hang of it soon. Soon you'll be keeping time with the rest of us, reading almost a thousand lines an hour..." But by Thursday he could feel himself left alone on the peninsula of the department. His cubicle was the last, a fuzzy pink edge before Design's stations cropped up beyond the border of the bathrooms — which, he noticed, seldom attracted passersby but had cubicle walls scratched full of dozens of names. It was as if, when the employees did visit, they were unable to resist an adolescent desire to leave their marks.

The Design Department was a land of men, mostly Asian. Gordon would glimpse them ducking in and out behind their masculine partitions — a set of blue cliffs. Gordon's work area was a virtual cabin of isolation, the floating green screen his life dinghy. Heroes and heroines traipsed across its face, then thrust their way to orgasm, tying the knot in less time than it had taken Gordon to secure the position at Heaven.

Gordon had been told there were more men on Floors Eighteen through Twenty-Three, Acquisitions and Substantive, but in his department on Floor Twelve there were only four men in a department of one hundred and thirty women — four men, and Gordon the only actual proofreader. There was Titus Bentley, Reception. There was Jon Manos, Proofreading supervisor and the department's flaming bon vivant — Gordon supposed Jon must be the only un-hetero person, place, or thing in the entire conservative company. There was Gordon himself, proofreading grunt and all-around-keeps-to-himself type. And "Daves," as he called himself, a lumberjack sort of guy whose first name and last name were apparently similar, some derivative of David — David Davies, or David Davidson

— Gordon couldn't remember. Daves worked in the one production office that bridged the gap between Proofreading and Design. Of the three — Bentley, Manos, and Daves — only Daves was friendly.

Jon Manos, whom Gordon had expected to give him kinder regard as a member of the slim minority of partway available men, stolidly reserved his better humour for the girls. Manos seemed to regard them as his own chorus line, kicking with commas instead of their legs, cloaked in red ink instead of red sequins. He was weedy for forty and had the same face Gordon could imagine him having had at fifteen. He wore pink or yellow polo shirts interchangeably with grey or brown vests, and a newsboy cap in the morning on his way in, peering out beneath it with crisp blue eyes that saw everything. He adored music and movies and spent more time discussing them in the corridor with whoever was passing by than he spent checking up on his staff's work. Occasionally Gordon got the impression that he was talking about pop culture items he himself hadn't seen or heard, but had only read about. In spite of what he and Gordon did not have in common, Gordon believed Manos would have been easy to get along with, interesting even, if he hadn't dismissed Gordon as a dud within the first second or two of his company orientation. He had been welcoming during Gordon's interview — all smiles up in Lillian Payne's office — but his manner down on Floor Twelve was another story. Here it was clear he viewed Gordon as little more than a grunt.

Manos rushed through the procedures, handed Gordon an assortment of forms, and left more every day or two with handwritten point-form instructions on how Gordon had mis-filed them and needed to redo them. There were time sheets, style sheets, telephone codes, and reading codes. The *time sheets* were not to be handed in to Manos directly but to be left at the end of every shift in a particular folder in an empty office at the end of the hall. The *style sheets* were to travel with the manu-scripts, no matter what. On them Gordon was to mark the spellings, the trademarks used throughout the stories, and the heroes' and heroines' names. The *telephone codes* were for his own use, so he could change his voice-mail message on a daily basis. He was reminded twice in the first week alone that he needed to do this if he expected to be paid for that day's hours. The voice-mail messages seemed to serve as a time clock or attendance system, and Gordon wondered who was checking them. The *reading codes* were to help him input corrections to the digital versions of the manuscripts, the documents that would be sent through to Design and Production when he was done with them, where they would be turned into layouts resembling books. These were essentially hot-key commands, although they seemed to Gordon to be anything but fast.

"Mr. Small," Manos said, leaning over Gordon's cubicle wall as Gordon scrolled ahead furiously to make it look as if he were reading faster than he was. "Watch your codes. Got a wee complaint about them." Manos held his finger and thumb an inch apart when he said "wee," but didn't elaborate on which codes, so Gordon simply nodded and scrolled on.

"You pack a PowerBar today, Jon?" one of the ladies called out to Manos, cruising by with a pink Adidas bag over one shoulder.

"Don't I every day?" Manos departed, having left a fresh pile of time sheets and memos on top of Gordon's inbox.

Already Gordon knew that Manos liked gym guys. During lunch hour he went cruising down on the sixth floor, where the weight room and treadmills were, and apparently had been with Heaven long enough that this was acceptable behaviour for a supervisor, and also acceptable cubicle conversation. Like everyone else, Gordon had overhead the stories Manos told to Gordon's colleagues Erika Workman and Jill Fast.

In contrast, Daves was the Grenwald of Heaven. He didn't gel his close-cropped hair and he didn't wear Adidas the way the mall's Champs manager did, but he had begun to drop by Gordon's cubicle to talk scores of games Gordon hadn't watched, or to silently punch Gordon's shoulder. Daves wore hiking shoes and plaid button-downs that his shoulders were threatening to break out of, perhaps an indication of what he did on his lunch, though whether he was one of the sixth-floor men that Manos cruised Gordon had no idea. "No worries," was Daves's favourite saying, and within a week of Gordon being at Heaven, Daves had already dropped it on him about sixty times. Daves was in his mid-twenties, about ten years younger than Gordon, and spent a lot of time walking around their department, passing out finished pages of the books they'd proofed as if he were passing around a bottle of something good. "Here, have a go at this," he'd command, slipping mocked-up covers salaciously into inboxes. Once already, Gordon had seen Daves actually whistle at Fiona Christiansen, who was a slim young married, and she had only smiled and wagged her finger at him like a 1950s schoolmarm. Gordon had been surprised to find out from One-Cubicle-Over Jill that

Daves was the last of eight children and lived with his seventy-four-year-old mother, whom he cared for. Grating though Daves' swaggering 100-percent can-do attitude could be, Gordon felt a little warmer toward him afterwards.

Then there were the women. Their names formed a list that Gordon attempted to access and replay as if it were the alphabet song. Every time a new one approached him, he ran through half the catalogue looking for the right descriptor. As soon as Gordon got to know them, the same way that Cinderella's carriage had turned back to a pumpkin, the women turned into little more than co-workers, into cousins of a sort. They wore skirts that touched their knees. They ate their lunches out of bags. They took the underground tunnel to go shopping on their lunch hour at the shoe outlet around the corner and came back tittering, lugging bulky black bags with mundane merchandise inside. They lowered their voices when they spoke of things menstrual, things maternal, or things to do with marriage. After the first couple of days Gordon made no attempt to listen. Quite simply, he and the rest of the department had made a mutual decision: Gordon was to be shut out of all things save those pertaining to spelling, punctuation, geographical queries, and quotations. It made no difference to him.

Gordon had already deduced that in the eight-hour day of romance, one could exist only in an asexual state. The ardour of the reading material left a taste in his mouth like old coffee. He hated to admit that he got strangely jacked up as Jessica Price — and she certainly had hers, a $10,000 gemstone bangle procured as easily as a packet of jujubes — jumped on Justin Prince, judiciously jiggled his johnson, felt its persuasive pulse, then let it all gap into hearts and gardenias, pleading with him to peer deep inside her to the little girl she had always been, and the woman she was still to be. The turn from excitation to exasperation was a blunt and sudden one. Gordon found himself scrolling ahead with juvenile eye-rolls. The arrow keys were his only friends. With crossed arms and tilted chins his subjects argued the arguments of dullards, then gave in, plunging and writhing and endlessly coming to release as Gordon's chair wheels ground into fireproof carpet. He didn't get hard so much as restless, an ongoing agitation settling over his lap like a winding sheet. All around him the office buzzed with faint, undefined tension. The proofreaders were as turned on as the fluorescent tubing overhead, but also as cold.

If he had thought that a job at Heaven would help him escape from the memory of his ex-wife, Chloe, Gordon couldn't have been more mistaken. In every romance there was room for the broken-hearted to mend her real relationship by replacing it momentarily with that of the character. And although he was a man reading these stories for women, he was not immune. Into their easy casings Gordon sandwiched himself and Chloe. It was not the Chloe he had parted from seven and a half years before that he imagined — it was the Chloe he'd begun with. A younger-than-he, wee, twee, twenty-three-year-old Chloe.

How ludicrous was it that her face should spring to his mind every time heroes and heroines kissed? They had practically "met cute." His first date with Chloe had been only a half-hour long. She'd phoned him two weeks after he passed her his number. It was suitably awkward: they discovered that she had a car and he did not, so she offered to drive. A day and time were arranged for "coffee and hanging out," whatever that meant. An hour later than she was supposed to arrive to pick him up, she phoned.

"Did we say we'd hang out tonight . . . ?" The words had slipped out of her mouth sounding sly and apologetic simultaneously, as if all the consonants were slanted sideways. Before he could reply she had amended, "I'm supposed to work. I could still swing by before my shift. We could do something quick, like coffee. Or Popsicles." In spite of his irritation at being half stood-up, the idea of eating Popsicles with a woman like Chloe had been extremely invigorating.

She picked him up in a rusted Firefly and whisked him off to a cappuccino place near the school for a date of only thirty-one minutes, including driving time. She apologized — she was meant to punch the clock at The Limited by 6 p.m. and not a minute later. "A three-hour shift," she complained. "It's not worth it." She sped past the pubs and falafel joints and diners and dollar stores with the accuracy of a motocross racer, secured the two of them cappuccinos, and arrived promptly back in front of the rented place he shared twenty-nine minutes later, where she said, "Can I give you a hug?" in spite of the digital time on the dashboard.

Her neck met his mouth when she one-armed him from the driver's seat. Even her one-armed hug was still a real hug, the kind that told him, *Hang on, you are loved, and even your squeezed breath is mine to love.*

Gordon scrolled ahead. He could feel the restlessness of Heaven around him as he read and remembered.

He could barely believe he had been bold enough to kiss her there, wetly, in the crook between her neck and her ear, and then apologize as he did it, to one side of her mouth, mumbling, "Sorry, you . . . smelled nice." Had he really said something so caveman-like and stupid? Chloe had laughed and he'd had to jump clear of the car as she revved down the street at a hug-and-kiss-delayed few minutes past the hour. She was supposed to be fourteen blocks away and already parked and punched. It was doomed from the start, he had snorted later, *a half-hour date*, the ridiculousness of their entire three-year relationship.

Now, in Heaven, it was as if Chloe and Gordon drank coffee together in the morning while he read about characters' first kisses. They kissed then too, dark-roast damp, lips like caramel cappuccino. Chloe sat behind Gordon as he ate lunch. She read over his shoulder about characters' family problems and insecurities — often obvious and relating to lack of fatherly love. Then in the afternoon, afternoon delight. A first fight at three o'clock. It wasn't easy to relive the downfall of his marriage in every week-long romance that came dancing across the screen. But it was inevitable. In every slight-waisted nymph Gordon saw Chloe in that button skirt eleven years before, her body less like an hourglass than a grenade. In every quivering pink nipple, areola of Chloe. In every wet, tight, wanting crux, eau de Chloe and Chloe alone.

It was a complete contradiction. Though Gordon had once slept beside this woman, touched this woman, smelled her, breathed her, exchanged matter with her, heard her occasional snoring or sneezing in the night, little remained but the crust of the emotion he associated with her. He knew that her first sexual experience had been with an older girl across the street, that she took her tea with milk and honey, that strawberries gave her hives, that she had weight issues and bought low-fat sour cream as if it could lessen her addiction, that she secretly loved disco, that she would wear black bras but not black underpants because she feared it would denote something distasteful about her. They were facts. Or they were now. Summaries of reality. The highs and lows. But the in-betweens were missing. He could remember the exact map her teeth made in her mouth, but if he tried to remember the salt of her skin, it evaporated beneath his memory's tongue.

THEN, ON FRIDAY, the woman was suddenly there. She was the first.

Gordon felt her before he saw her. He could sense her long, dark eyelashes going blink-blink over the partition.

Gordon turned and — blink-blink — there she was. "Hi . . ." he mumbled, physically indexing his brain by pressing a pair of searching fingertips to his left temple.

"Erika," she supplied. "Workman."

"Erika Workman." Gordon wagged his finger at her.

She quickly scooted from her perch — where, a fraction of a second before, one elbow had hooked over the cubicle wall — to the inside of Gordon's not-so-vast workspace.

"Is it a truism?" she whispered.

"Is what a truism?"

She was leaning forward. To compensate, Gordon leaned

backwards in his chair. The wheels yelped. If it weren't for her proximity he would have assumed she had come for what they all came for: advice about straightening out some maxim or misquote. She was one of the youngest, her cheeks still puffed with dorm-room cider. There was a blemish along her jaw that had not vanished in the week Gordon had been at Heaven, but her eyes were absolute amber and her collarbone was incomparable. Blink.

"You know what they're saying?"

"You want help with a saying?"

Blink. "No." A blue and yellow set of breasts pressed against a cotton T as she leaned closer.

"What *they're* saying," she hissed through a small black gap in her front teeth. Her lips were the colour of penny candy. Gordon clutched *Webster's* across his lap like a shield. She rolled her eyes slowly to indicate some presence beyond his head, beyond the cubicle. "What they're saying, is it true?"

Nothing to do with a truism at all. What was it they were saying? Gordon shook his head, let *Webster's* slip a bit as Erika retreated a few inches. She set up camp on the corner of his desk, her denim skirt hitching up almost above the kneecap. One red sneaker dangled, its small suede body notched with brand. She was less churchy than the others, Gordon saw now. Her youth permitted her wardrobe to be more casual. She wore burgundy trouser socks, in spite of the skirt, and above them — that gulping patella as she let the red shoe swing. Back. Forward. Gordon's eyes followed. When he looked up at her face again, she had turned her head away, was peering off over the cubicle's top, on lookout as she waited for his answer.

"I — I don't know what this is about. Are you sure it has to do with me?"

She ducked her brown head. "No . . . no." Blink-blink. "It has to do with Chloe Gold."

Somewhere in Design a book toppled to the floor. An outdated scanner slammed shut. A neon band of pain formed behind Gordon's brow.

"Oh . . . Chloe." At that moment the computer terminal went to sleep, and in its dark face Gordon could see himself visibly grimace.

"So you *know* her."

"I know her," he confirmed, the three words a more complex sentence than any he had edited so far.

"You. Know. *Chloe. Gold.*" Erika Workman's voice jumped an octave with each word. The heel of her red shoe kicked the desk drawer, slamming it on its spring. The shoe swung haphazardly around the cubicle and Gordon desperately wondered how he could turn his pain to his advantage. Erika's exposed kneecap was a porcelain pitcher of cream. Gordon loathed hearing his wife's name parked next to such enthusiasm. But everything about Erika Workman was suddenly bobbing. "Chloe Gold, the *Goodbye to the Wind* author?" Erika leaned in so close that Gordon wondered if he should take cover again beneath the *Webster's*. She wriggled ass-backwards so the desk supported her full weight, placed her hands on her bare knees, both feet off the floor now. "*The* Chloe Gold. So it is a truism?"

"No," he said, "but it's true." He nodded, slowly, reluctantly. "She was my wife."

"She's your —"

"*Ex* —"

"— wife."

"— wife."

"Oh! Snap! Jinx!" Erika cheered, and sprang from the desk, denim down again. She put her finger to her lips — blink-blink — and tore away.

BEFORE WHOOPSY'S ON DUFFERIN Avenue there had been the office on Bond Street.

In the office on Bond, Gordon had read manuscripts for Dr. Greer Black, at a literary magazine known simply as *post–*. He'd been fresh out of university and hadn't even met Chloe yet. Dr. Black kept the manuscripts in apple boxes and banker's boxes and paid Gordon $100 for each carton he emptied. Gordon went in for ten hours a week to read them. They came from all over — from the inhabitants of little islands in British Columbia that had no electricity; university grads teaching English in China, Korea, France, Sweden; farmwives suffocating on dust in Middle America; activists building schools in Peru; hockey coaches in factory towns who fancied themselves poets; and the sad pathetic souls, like Gordon, who had every faculty available to them for careers in literature but who couldn't step far enough outside themselves to see that what they had set down on the page was little more than an undergrad diary written with the assistance of a thesaurus. "Don't read — just skim," Dr. Black told him. "You'll never get through them otherwise. It'll break your heart, it's so hilarious."

She was right. There were stories about husbands and wives who had gone missing from one another, then reunited only to share long, tragically boring marriages. There were illustrated cat and dog stories by adults burning with desire to be *auteurs* and *artistes*, who hadn't studied either writing or drawing since sixth grade and didn't understand why Gordon and Dr. Black wouldn't accept their "graceful line renderings" and reproduce them in full colour. Pencil-crayoned dogs eating ice-cream cones married blue-Bic cats who held funerals for great-aunts with eating disorders, who were succeeded by adopted Chinese daughters, whose mothers went missing in small-town murder mysteries where cops hid their homosexual urges under heterosexual teen porn rings but wound up exposed by meddlesome academics with degrees in medieval literature and Japanese studies, who sat gazing from windows at leaves changing colour while remembering first loves they had played doctor with in root cellars, who wound up as thrift-conscious double divorcees, who wound up as cross-country-cycling swingers, who wound up as spiritual leaders, who wound up as pot-promoting grandparents, who wound up dying of colon cancer (or lung cancer or leukemia or AIDS), finally inducted into the Football Hall of Fame and leaving behind three manuscripts: one on financial planning, one of poetry (in spite of an inability to name a single poet living or dead), and one about the relationship between women and cats and men and dogs.

By the year's end that little office on Bond was broken, rejection slips scattered across Gordon's desk, still unmailed. He had worked with Dr. Black for eleven months and done

away with only four apple boxes. According to the Manuscripts Status logbook, Gordon had broken exactly 294
hearts. In the hallway six more boxes awaited his tearful gaze.
They couldn't have it. It wasn't fair. Gordon began opening
manila envelopes and shoving the forms in without so much
as a glance. Grandfathers of famous dancers now living in
Ukraine would put down their pens and stop chronicling as a
result of Gordon's carelessness. High school students with
crushes on aging literary figures would turn off their computers, dye their hair black, and take up with Marilyn Manson
instead. Master's grads with bad habits in black-and-white
photography and rhyming poetry would switch to cocaine
and nightclubs.

Even now, in Gordon's room on Russet Avenue, beneath
the bed, there was still one last box, the one that had gone
missing. Gordon had moved it three times because he hadn't
been able to bring himself to put them out on the street, those
works. Good or bad, each belonged to someone, and he had
imagined their aspiring authors coincidentally tripping by his
recycling bin some rainy night, only to catch sight of their
own title pages staring up at them. The box of broken dreams
had been collecting dust for ten years, sleeping beneath the
space where Gordon slept.

post– was spelled intentionally with a dash and without a
capital letter. It was an offshoot literary journal from Gordon's
alma mater, and Dr. Black was the only editor. She had, in fact,
been the only editor, with the exception of a transient team of
students, since 1974. The journal was an oddity, published
twice yearly in hardcover — which was a large part of its

appeal to up-and-coming writers. To be published in hard-cover was somehow better than soft, in spite of *post–*'s obvious lack of newsstand presence. An acceptance to *post–* meant yes, you had made it. Merely by digging through the manuscript boxes then, by extension, Gordon had made it. The summer that Gordon cleared out all six apple boxes in four weeks, Dr. Black agreed to publish one of the three stories he had managed to bang out — the shortest one, she decided in the end.

He was twenty-five years, two months, and two days old when *Gordon Small* appeared in cursive on the cover in a long list of other names of would-be writers. *post–*: ed. Dr. Greer Black; contributors: Chloe Gold, Gordon Small. The twenty or so other names in the 10-point font had since faded into the weave of the cover. Chloe's poem was about flowers, tricks you could play on them. It was short and fidgety, full of word play and irregular line breaks. But good, Gordon thought, maybe. He could tell, the first time he read the poem, long before it appeared in print, that Chloe would be pretty.

The day *post–* had arrived from the printer, the office on Bond Street had swirled with the scent of ink toxins. Curlicues of Styrofoam had floated across the scarred production table. The sunlight had lilted across the sixty-pound paper stock that was *post–*'s trademark. Sections of someone else's misprinted books had been stuffed, like black-and-white-striped pillows, inside the edges of *post–*'s boxes to keep their Gordon-Small–adorned covers from dinging against the sides. It was glorious, they were glorious, they were *post–*glorious. Dr. Black had held one up, squinted at it, and said, "Today, *post–*, tomorrow, post-*post–*," as if there were anything else to go on to.

Gordon had gone home that day, taken a shower, and lain on his bed. He had been able to hear his roommate through the rented nicotined walls, unaware, attempting to play Zeppelin's "Tangerine" on an acoustic guitar to Susan or Janey. Gordon had closed his eyes, and Susan *and* Janey had joined him on his newly published side of the wall.

He'd met Chloe Gold two weeks later, at the September launch of *post–*. She hadn't been as pretty as he'd imagined, but she was one of only three women who had been published in the fall *post–*. Not only that, she'd had every confidence that Gordon was going to be the country's next big thing. As always she'd been close enough to the truth to be worth believing: in the following year he'd pumped out an ultra-slim novel with a small press whose publisher was friendly with Dr. Black. The book had been printed on cheap paper and given the kind of marketing afforded a new style of gyro at a Greek restaurant. But on this particular night, belief had been all that mattered. The university faculty lounge had a balcony running all the way around it, complete with moon, and Chloe was wearing a black fringed shawl and a skirt with buttons like upturned blue eyeballs.

Gordon was sure Heaven had accepted him because he had managed to stretch his ten-hour-per-week *post–* experience into a virtual lifetime of work before he'd been sidetracked by "research" for a second novel set in the Dufferin neighbourhood. After all, he was the very first editor to select a piece for publication by the best-selling Chloe Gold.

Her name now appeared in his mind in uppercase foil letters. It shook him to remember the modesty of Chloe's youth

— its lowercased initials — and the days before he had begun dreaming of her funeral. Gordon was not the type of man to daydream-plan murder so much as the kind to envision a million possible scenarios for accidental death, flowers and elegies, the consolations of Chloe's attractive sister, television interviews, his own comeback, and remarriage.

THEY ALL VISITED HIS CUBICLE after that. Gordon was Heaven's minor celebrity. They came from Proofreading, Copy Editing — even Hello Sonja from Foreign Rights came, bringing her screensaver face with her. One of the men journeyed over from Design. He had to know, he whispered, was she really all that? Gordon leaned back in his chair, arms veed behind his head, and, strangely, enjoyed his newfound fame. In all his time at the mall, no one had ever asked about his personal life. There had been shoppers, even other mall employees, who must have known who Chloe Gold was, despite the mall's obvious deficiency in books. But if those knowing souls existed, they had stayed on the other side of the line separating Whoopsy's from the mall walkways, perhaps repelled by the television merchandise that surrounded Gordon. Besides, the wedding ring had made its way from his finger to his sock drawer, and Gordon had donned a shield of anonymity along with his Whoopsy's golf shirt.

She was, Gordon said, all *that*, and he grinned at his own falsity, at the ease with which he had what others now wanted. The man, who had eyes like wilted cucumber, went away firm and crisp with hope. He'd given Gordon a look-over — the new suit now creased with daily wear — and had seen that Gordon was khaki, unironed, plain and brown in a pair of nearly sole-less shoes. He'd sprung up, shaking Gordon's hand as if it were the hammer for the strongman's bell at a fairground.

GORDON STARED AT THE KETTLE in the lunchroom. Wisps were coming out of it like spittle off a dog's tongue in summer. It didn't whistle, he'd learned the hard way, and he would be reprimanded if he went away and left it. He'd been told that someone had brought it in from home and they weren't sup-posed to have it in the first place. The staff had been warned to be particularly careful with the few privileges they'd stolen.

Georgianne Bitz came into the kitchen and took a tuna-fish sandwich out of the refrigerator. She held it like a dead thing. She went to the cupboard and took out a white plate that had her name on it in sparkly red paint. She cautiously laid the waxed paper parcel on the plate, between the G and the E. The letters were coagulated like old blood on either side of the tuna corpse. Gordon could see it had been cut down the cen-tre after being wrapped — a white surgical incision. She stared at it, then at him.

"What's wrong?" asked Gordon.

"What do you have?"

"Tea, but not yet." Gordon pointed to the renegade kettle.

"Trade you."

He shrugged. The kettle began to lisp. He went back to his cubicle with GEORGIANNE in nail-polish letters beneath his thick thumbs.

The hero had forgotten condoms. Then he remembered the one his friend had insisted he keep — as a joke. But he and the woman of his dreams were camping. A raccoon had gotten into their personal items. He chased the raccoon in spite of his erection. "Come back here," he hollered. The woman rolled about on the bed, laughing until she cried. When he retrieved it, tricking it away from the raccoon, the condom was still in its package. He leaned in the doorway, suavely, nakedly. "Guess what I have for you . . ." "Whatever it is, it had better be long and it had better be hard." She had never been so shameless in her life. But looking at him standing there, she could think of nothing to stop her. It was he who was making her this way. It was — oh my God, it couldn't be — *love* for him that was making her behave this way. As he joined with her, penetrating her to her core, waves of capital-L *Love* washed over her. It was! It was love!

Georgianne Bitz brought back Gordon's empty cup. It was blue, with a sea-green band around the top. He handed her the plate.

"Who makes the sandwiches?"

"My kid. Jolene. She's eight."

Georgianne and Jolene. Gordon thought they ought to be working a vegetable stand together, somewhere in Nebraska. "If you don't like tuna fish, can't you teach her peanut butter?"

"Jo likes tuna. She thinks she's doing me a favour. How can I say no?"

Georgianne was tall and toothy. When she spoke, her mouth moved like a horse's. Gordon thought of Mr. Ed. Ms. Ed. She laughed. He smiled.

"You got a raw deal. A sandwich for a tea?"

"I know."

Gordon looked into his cup. She had washed it. He hadn't washed her plate. A halo of dark brown hair floated away over the tops of the cubicles. It was curled like an old lady's, even though Georgianne was only a few years older than him. Thirty-nine or forty, forty-four tops. Gordon watched it go like some frothed-up chocolate ice-cream shake. She was nice. When he turned back to the hero and heroine, they were already engaged. They had done it two more times — without condoms. That rascally raccoon was cheering them from the cabin window. The lady was having his baby, but hadn't told him yet. Gordon moved the mug to various positions around his desk. Georgianne was the first woman in two weeks to enter his cubicle without using the toll-bridge token of his ex-wife's name. He put the cup to his nose and smelled it. Sunlight.

5

TITUS BENTLEY'S DESK was stacked with boxes, the paper lips of envelopes emerging from the tops, each biting the one next to it.

"Morning..." Gordon hustled by, eager to get his computer switched on, set his voice mail for the day, and head for the kitchenette with its coffee urn and chance of exchange with Georgianne Bitz. Once the computer's dumb skull was illuminated, he considered himself officially at work.

Above the propped-up house of invoice cards, Bentley returned his gaze with distrust. "Morning..."

Bentley's was the first desk one came to before reaching the Proofreading Department. In Gordon's opinion Bentley smelled of Elmer's glue. So far as Gordon could discern, he was Reception. Though whom he received Gordon was unsure. As a rule they didn't speak. Or at least they hadn't thus far. Normally Gordon nodded or shuffled past shyly. They had been introduced once, on Gordon's first day, amid Gordon's initiation into telephone extensions and reading codes. Bentley had had incredibly cold hands when they shook. Just as Manos had done, he had assessed Gordon quickly, thin face splitting with a smile that was more a baring of teeth. He was as tall as the Thin Man, and about as welcoming too. It was as though it was a requirement in this environment that the men regard one another with bristling ferocity, territorial callousness.

Titus Bentley held a weird grimace in place following his "Morning . . ." At six feet four he would have towered over Gordon even more if he hadn't had a self-conscious stoop to accompany his livery lips and penetrating black-hole eyes. Bentley's hair swooped over his forehead like a dead crow, a tuft sticking up in the back just before the halo of baldness. His eyes narrowed as he watched Gordon, as though he hated him intensely for no reason but Gordon's existence. At that very moment — and every moment Gordon could recall being in his presence — Bentley seemed as though he were thinking of twisting Gordon's neck like an old grease rag.

In spite of himself, Gordon hurried past Titus Bentley, muscles in his throat constricting. At his cubicle Gordon tossed his jacket over his hook, snapped on his computer, and headed for the kitchen. Partway there he turned and headed back to his workstation. He had forgotten his coffee mug. He ground his front teeth together. He hated himself for his fear. Bentley was just a scrawny, vertically surplused freak. He thought he owned the department only because he owned Reception. Gordon could say "Good morning" every day if he wanted. In fact he would, he promised himself, if only to irritate Bentley. Gordon grabbed his Georgianne-graced cup so quickly that it rolled off the desk. He caught it before it could hit the carpet.

Gordon pushed the door to the kitchen hard, practically hitting Georgianne Bitz, who was carrying her own mug — *I Heart Mom* — full to the brim. "Oooh!" She jumped back, a small burp of black coffee escaping the rim and falling between them. "Fu-dge," she blurted, a mom-style obscenity. "Did I get you?"

Gordon shook his head. "Sorry."

They cantered around, he trying to politely extricate himself from her path and she turning and heading back to the counter, where she freed a square of paper towel. She wiped around her cup with no-nonsense efficiency. "What's up, Gord?"

He shrugged, moved toward the coffee urn reluctantly. He pressed the lever and filled, Colombian Supremo, while she leaned back against the counter staring at him. There was one other guy in the kitchen — Design — and one of the token Design women, small and dark-eyed. She and Gordon exchanged glances, like strangers sharing some brief moment of affinity. But ultimately all Designs were alien to Gordon, and Proofreadings to them. Even now the two moved around each other, plucking cream from the same fridge, sugar from the same cupboard, without speaking, another language separating them. The Designs' was one of pixillation, RGB/CMYK, JPEG/TIFF; Gordon's and Georgianne's was comprised of single quotes, double quotes, solidi, commas, colons, question marks, exclamation points. It was early yet, 8:32 by the microwave clock. Georgianne and Gordon could talk freely here.

"You ever start the day in a perfect mood?" he asked. "One thing happens and you're thrown off?"

Georgianne gave an exaggerated tight-lipped grin, cocked a finger on her free hand at her coffee mug.

"Oh, I see." He blushed. Chloe had once told Gordon that he was incredibly cute when he blushed. But given his height, and Georgianne's, he was certain he looked like a squat stuffed apple.

"Kidding, *kid*-ding." She put on a fake fast-talking voice, slightly misty, semi-Southern. "Who was it? You want, I'll take 'em to task. Say the word, Gord. I always carry a pearl-handled revolver in my purse."

Impossible, coming from a woman with hands wrapped around *I Heart Mom*, the hollow skin beneath her eyes pink as plucked chicken. Was he insane?

"Thin Man. He's a mean one. Mean as tomorrow." Gordon looked to see if it would land.

"Ugh, Titus," Georgianne groaned, making a fairly unattractive sound in the back of her throat even as she smiled. "Be glad you aren't a woman — he's even worse." She wrinkled her nose, gave Gordon a wink, and backed out of the kitchen, using her bum to open the two-way door before he could ask her what she'd brought for lunch.

She had a kid, maybe a husband, and she was too farmwife in the looks department for Gordon. She'd given him a sandwich and a laugh, but nothing more. He chided himself for seeking an office romance so early in his new job. Whoopsy's had done something to him, he told himself — buried him under a set of not-for-the-parlour games while Chloe had become more and more distant, rising behind him like an evening star.

Jill Fast trucked into the kitchen and depressed the coffee lever and claimed the sugar bowl simultaneously, as if the Designs couldn't be trusted with it. She called to Gordon cheerily, "Get your pay?" Stationed one cubicle over from Gordon, Jill was in her late twenties, with straight blond bangs and brown dog-eyes, but a tendency to bite. Given the generosity of her lower half, she wore her clothes a shade too snug. Gordon could always see her panty lines. She gave off the insecure air of the prom queen's best friend.

He shook his head.

"Well, today's the day!" she sang. "Is it your first?"

Nod.

"When you first start, they make you wait. Talk to Titus."

Gordon gritted his teeth against the rim of his cup, hid his scowl by tipping it into the heat of the brew. Millstone. "Bentley?"

"Yeah, *duh* . . ." Jill's sweetness ran out quickly. She released the sugar bowl and slithered out.

THE FOYER HAD A WAN LIGHT, a different fluorescence than the rest of Heaven.

Titus Bentley had dry patches on his palms, flakes of loose skin around his knuckles, and nails like dried wallpaper paste. As he crab-walked his scruffy mitts through the *S*'s, an indignant heat rose in Gordon's cheeks. "Oh, *that's* right," Bentley drawled, as if he had just remembered. It was obvious that whatever he was about to reveal he had known before Gordon had even said "good morning." "You're not here yet."

Bentley huffed and shrugged, lurching his shoulders. "Still temp."

Gordon fixed him with his best blank glare.

"All Heaven employees are on contract for their first two months." Bentley peered from beneath his birdlike brow. Even when he dripped sympathy, he looked like he wanted to crack Gordon's spine. "It was in your contract. Or didn't you read it?"

"When do I get paid?"

Bentley made a stalling sound in the back of his throat, drawing out Gordon's suffering as long as possible. "You can't pick it up here . . ." *Ta-ta-ta.* "But you're paid already . . ." *Ta-ta-ta.* "You'll have to go over to . . ." *Ta-ta-ta.* "Job City."

"Well, where's that?" Gordon felt himself becoming petulant. He hated having his time wasted — especially his lunch hour — by one as reptilian as Bentley.

Bentley closed his file box. "It's in your contract." He smiled, teeth like pinheads.

GORDON FOUND GEORGIANNE BITZ'S cubicle, wedged into the farthest possible corner from his. Her chocolate-Coke hairdo fizzed up above the pink fuzzy walls. Gordon stood behind her, regarding the back of her neck. He leaned into the cubicle, one hand balanced on the divider.

"Where's Job City?" he whispered.

She spun in her chair in alarm, a pair of horn-rims decorating her nose. *I Heart Mom* sat empty on the desk beside a cardboard cup of soup. "Twice in one day . . . Don't *do* that!" She snagged a Kleenex from the box, wiped her tomato lips, and hit the garbage basket with it on the first shot. "What do you need?"

"Job City."

"Right. That's what it was — with Titus." She set her glasses on the desk, jabbed her thumbs between her eyes, her head down. "How to get there . . ."

"Is it far?"

"No, no, right around the corner, but . . . How can I describe it? It's been so long since I had to go there. Telling you would be like trying to give precise directions to my high school." Gordon thought about interjecting some flattering comment dubious of her age, but decided against it. She closed her eyes again. "I can see it, but it's like a dream. Okay, here's what you'll do. Take the elevator all the way down to the basement —"

"The basement?"

"The first basement, not the second basement —"

"What's the second basement?"

"Parking garage. First basement, follow the arrows through the passage —"

"The passage?"

"It's what the girls take. Every time they go for shoes. You know, *the Passage*. It goes underneath."

"Well, can't I just go outside? It's nicer."

She turned her chair toward the window and, lips slack, stared through the tinted glass across the expanse of concrete. A bra and underwear manufacturer's logo made an orange stick-figure splash against their parking lot. The sky was overcast but bright. A burning bush shed small red leaf-petals in a perfect circle on the grass. It was a hollow, floating morning, the day still trying to figure out what it wanted to be. They both looked up and down the expanse.

"The thing is . . ." Georgianne's voice faltered. "I don't know how." She pointed to the curving roadway, in the direction from which the bus had brought him to Heaven. "It's back that way," she said, her voice thimble-sized. "That's all I know." Her shoulders sank into the rose tweed of the swivel chair.

"It's okay," Gordon told her. "I'll take the Passage."

She gave him the instructions. Blue arrow to red arrow, red arrow to yellow. Left underneath Nine West, past the glass doors of Print Three, and after that either the first or second door on the right. Job City. It would be labelled, she said.

When Gordon left Georgianne, she still had a faraway look in her eyes. She moved the computer screen around until there was no reflection in it. He noticed, glancing back, that she stood up and twisted the blinds closed anyway.

AS HE WALKED TO THE ELEVATORS, past Bentley's podium, Bentley put a hand up to detain Gordon. "Small?"

Gordon waited, but Bentley wasn't looking at him. His eyes were searching the second shelf of his station.

"Small?"

Gordon sighed, answered him with a sarcastic schoolboy's "Yes . . . ?"

"You'll need one of these, won't you?" Bentley opened a miniature brown envelope and took out an oblong tab of black plastic.

With recognition and defeat, the word blipped out again. "Yes . . ."

It was a security card. For weeks Gordon had been signing in and out with the cow-eyed guard in the lobby, entry authorized by others, riding down with co-workers.

Bentley put the access card back in its coin envelope and slid it to Gordon across the wooden stand. Gordon picked it up only after Bentley's hands had left it, as if they were sharing a woman. The tiny envelope had his name written across it in a flowing female hand: *For Gordon Small, Urgent.*

"This mine?"

"Lily just sent it down for you."

Gordon didn't like the way he said Lillian's name. *Lily.* Like it was something he could hold between his pasty thumbs.

"That's HR," Bentley continued. "Nothing's important until they think it is. They could take a week or a month or a year to get you all approved and firmed up."

Gordon didn't like the way he said *firmed up* either.

"Thanks." Gordon edged away from Bentley, still looking down at the object.

The plastic had a nice, compact, solid feel in his palm, like a dark, sand-polished skipping stone. Gordon ran his thumb over the loops and eyes of Lillian Payne's handwriting before tucking the empty envelope in his pocket, safe against his groin. He hit the elevator with his new status, swiped himself for the first time, and watched the panel colour change. Like a rainbow. Gordon was official at Heaven. He held his own disco in the steel box as he dropped — thirteen storeys.

6

GORDON HELD THE STUB of his cheque aloft — the statement that alerted him that the company had made the most recent instant deposit. "Hello, my pet," he said to the paper tongue. He fed it to his wallet like a dog treat and turned from his inbox to his telephone. Though he never visited the teller, Gordon was developing a simple and satisfying relationship with his bank account. Settling in at Heaven meant he no longer saw the inside of the bank. Or a grocery store or pharmacy for that matter.

When he checked his office voice mail, he found two messages from his co-worker Ivy Wolfe.

One: "Eden Eats has arrived, Gordon!"

Two: "Ivy again. Noticed you had some yogourt. Didn't want that to turn inside out on you, so I've stashed it in the Net fridge. Venture up when you can."

Within days of his Chloe Gold status circulating, the romantics and the granola heads had found him. Ivy was one of these, and when she said the word "Net," her voice lifted ever so slightly. It was just a blip really, but to Gordon it spoke volumes about Heaven's Internet Division. Ivy and her fellow Floor Fifty-Eight workers seemed to believe their department was the mecca of Heaven. The word always fell from their lips with a certain reverence. Whenever Gordon journeyed up to collect his groceries, he noticed that she and her co-workers lounged and twisted in their backless chairs as if they were practising yoga while typing.

Ivy was a chickpea-coloured politico who farted liberally — small vegetarian drafts smelling strangely of A1 Steak Sauce — and Gordon wondered if he should have trusted her. She had approached him to explain that there was an all-organic online grocery service that — if he were willing to join with her and several others in a group order — would save Gordon substantial amounts. He could schlep his food home from there, she had insisted, or, if he preferred, order only what he needed for his lunches. Previously Gordon's shopping habits had tended toward the bigger and better. His grocery cart at the mall had always been loaded with Hungry-Man Sports Grill meals, which required no grill at all, just a spin of the microwave dial. Pre-Heaven, even his toothpaste had been turbo — Max Fresh. When the woman on the packaging opened her mouth, little icicle stars tumbled out. *iCouldwin*, Gordon's cola case had declared, though he'd known he never would. Gordon had let Ivy sign him up, agreeing only out of sheer sloth. In the mornings he ate at the break-room table, masticated apricot granola and suckled on rice milk or strawberry soy. In a matter of days a new lifestyle had been built.

Eating all-organic did something funny to Gordon. Although he didn't feel bunged up, some days he couldn't remember the last time he'd seen the inside of the men's room. Was this health? He needed to increase his bran intake, he decided. He went searching down in the concourse — or Passage, as the girls called it — for a raisin muffin. He found a corner outlet called Muffins Don't Grow on Trees, and sadly it was true. There was a counter girl there with a paper hat perched upon dark curls. She had an incredibly long nose and an equally wide smile for Gordon. But the glass domes of all four muffin trays were empty, protecting only an array of brown and yellow crumbs. Brownies she had in abundance. Butter croissants. Brittle horns of cannoli. Cinnamon twists. Almond biscotti. Peach tarts glazed so thick the fruit appeared plastic. And old-fashioned granny-like scones that looked as though they had been dropped from a great height, landed, and hardened — plain, cheese, and cheese and ham. The aroma of the place almost did Gordon in. He contemplated a vanilla ladyfinger, but in the end he ducked his head into his shirt collar and the paper-hat girl smiled wider, self-consciously, as he turned and fled.

Chloe had been a baker who refused to eat her own concoctions. Instead, she broke them into very small pieces and nibbled mouselike on them. Going empty-handed to friends' houses or family gatherings was to Chloe like wearing one's clothes inside out and backwards. She would rather be two hours late and proudly present a waxed-paper package over the doorstep. She would make things and leave Gordon at home with them while they cooled, sometimes for hours.

When she returned, she would always beam at Gordon —
"Ate them all, did you?" — and rub his belly as if he were a
Buddha figure and could grant her luck. He almost became fat
while living with her. He gained ten pounds in the first year.
Chloe began to refer to him as *man* rather than *boy*. She argued
with herself about her tendency toward feminism and this
strange urge to make things, to mince, whisk, roll, fold, sprinkle, grate, drop, frost. "Aprons," she spat like a curse. She had
five. She always smelled of cinnamon and vanilla, praline. Her
mouth, however, was anything but. When Gordon kissed her
on baking days, there were often traces of cigarettes he hadn't
seen her smoke. She tasted crisp, burnt. He wondered if
beneath his thumbs she would crumble at the edges.

Later, after he'd started managing Whoopsy's, he would
walk past the new and irksome Cinnabon store twice a day. Its
homemade perfume wafted nine stores in either direction.
Each time he passed — six years, six and a half, seven years
after they had parted ways — he thought of Chloe. He knew it
was wrong that she had lodged in his brain like an unrequited
love, but that was just it. She was elusive. Like a girl he'd never
had, even when he'd had her. Chloe: sometimes sandalwood
but always cinnamon. When he smelled it, she infused his
thoughts for an hour, sometimes twelve.

Gordon rounded the Passage corner and put Muffins Don't
Grow on Trees out of view behind him, pressing the Up button seven times in quick succession. There was a different
kind of granola available through Eden Eats, and he made a
mental note to order it next time. Fruit too.

OVER THE PAST FEW WEEKS Gordon's life had become such a streamlined, insular shuttle he hadn't even noticed going to work and back to his door. He was surprised one evening to round the corner of Russet Avenue and find Grenwald's sticky head bopping between the columns on the Ashbridge porch. It was obvious that no one had answered Grenwald's knock, which was quite unusual. Gordon could not think where Mrs. Ashbridge could be. Though she had her morning groups, by this time of day his landlady was usually there, on the porch. To see his old mall buddy in her place was quite alarming. Grenwald was clearly agitated, in a way Gordon had seen only when Grenwald was bested by west-end youth, clubbed down by slang he did not know or unable to figure out exactly who had snatched that last Nike-swooshed shirt, tucked it into their pants, and made off with it gratis. Grenwald actually paced.

It dawned on Gordon that instead of walking up and greeting his friend, he had unconsciously stopped a short distance away. He put his hand on the tree beside him. With the exception of the Brass Taps and their daily bucket o' beer, Gordon had never seen Grenwald outside of work. Always with the intention of approaching, Gordon observed.

With the pivot characteristic of a five-foot-seven salesman of sporting goods, Grenwald swung around the brick veranda. Instead of a basketball he had his keys, which busied one hand. He bounced them on a chain. The other hand was engaged in buttoning a telephone number into his cell. Though it was only six at night, it emitted a tetragon of blue from its mechanical face. Gordon was accustomed to Grenwald's need to jabber away to one unfortunate girl or another, but this time

Grenwald held the phone low to his chin and spoke directly into its mouthpiece as if he were issuing short-wave-radio directives rather than pillow musings. Then he did something highly atypical: he stopped speaking. He pressed the phone to his ear and stood staring so intently in Gordon's direction that Gordon found himself stepping behind the tree. When he looked again, Grenwald had ended the call. For a moment he stood looking down into his palm, where the gadget lay. His thinking face. He pocketed the phone.

Grenwald strode out into the street and stood looking up at Gordon's attic window. His back straightened as if he were taking a deep breath. Gordon could see it in his shoulders, the way they spread, fluid, backwards, the white jacket collecting up the last remaining strands of light and letting them run off like water. Up in the window a black suit bag stood watch. Gordon didn't know if Grenwald could see it from where he stood, but he imagined he could, because Gordon suddenly had an eerie feeling, recollecting its shape where it hung against the closet door. Gordon didn't even need to squint to see it.

A hunter green compact sped up the one-way street in the wrong direction. The driver seemed to express no hesitation about the decision, and parked, still facing the wrong direction, at the end of Mrs. Ashbridge's walk. Some men know a woman from a great distance by the way she stands or walks; Gordon knew her by the way she drove. Before a leg ending in a no-nonsense Clarks shoe had emerged from the driver's side, Gordon had begun pulling chunks of bark from the tree that hid him, tearing the coarse matter with his fingernails.

Above a basic white blouse and jeans belted with an olive scarf, Chloe's cinnamon hair floated across the lawn. Her age was like a medallion around her neck. Her eyes were smudged with fatigue, creased at the corners in a way Gordon did not remember. She was not the woman he had known but rather some sort of sophisticated or graduate version, a woman with all the paperwork to claim she was Chloe — to the extent that even Gordon was impressed. Grenwald extended his hand, but Chloe clasped him instead in a quick hug. It was fast but expressive, and the sleeve fell back from Chloe's forearm as she removed it from Grenwald's neck.

Gordon ran his hand through his hair, but it felt like wood. He looked down at his hands. He had broken his nails on the tree bark without feeling it. He did something then that he didn't understand, even as it happened. Gordon turned and fled.

He sprinted toward the neighbour's backyard, through it, past the marble-eyed cat, into the yard of the next house, down its walk and into Pauline Avenue, up Pauline, and back around to Bloor, landing on his toes, footsteps ringing light as pins. He broke hard left, put the Indian dollar store behind him, the Portuguese bakery, the Islamic mosque, the Baptist church — *At the heart of every conflict is a selfish heart* — and swung down the subway stairs.

Later, rattling northward, head *tut-tut-tut*ting against the Pantene Pro-V poster that promised longer, stronger hair and 100 percent more shine enhancement, Gordon still didn't know why he had reacted as he did. A thousand images nabbed him. He recalled Chloe at a book signing, though he was sure he had never attended one. Vividly the cover was shutting under her hand, then there was another book, another cover opened, another cover shut. He recalled the empty whisky glass on his bedside table. Why these images held such weight and why they should come at him now, he couldn't say.

He rose and exited the car at the next stop. Gordon's hands shook as he strode along the platform. He stopped for a moment. He closed his eyes. It was just a hug. Chloe hugged everyone. It was just a sleeve. Gordon saw it falling back again. Unplanned though it was, he saw the moment again, made more intimate by that glimpse of flesh so late in the fall. How had Chloe and Grenwald ever met? He tried to remember if he had ever told Grenwald about her. He hadn't, he was certain he hadn't. But what were they doing there on his porch? Waiting for him? Gordon took another step. A cautious step. Then he put his head down and sprinted up the subway station stairs, intending to cross over and come down on the other side, ride the seven stops back to his neighbourhood, and find out what had happened on Russet Avenue; why Grenwald was boomeranging around the porch; why Chloe, after eight years' absence, was suddenly shooting down his street of crabapples, clipping shears, and quiet; why Gordon himself had felt that odd impulse to flee. But at the top of the stairs something stopped Gordon in his tracks.

Two-dimensional swirls of pink and taffy chenille, layers of metallic ink:

CHLOE GOLD.
Go Deeper.
The award-winning author

brings you her long-awaited Hello Twilight,
a tale of romance and murder that demands to know:
how do you say farewell to a love already gone?

Her name in trademark all-caps, Chloe stood, beyond life-size, leaning against a fence made of driftwood, a different scarf than the one he had just seen her wearing, this one coffee-coloured, half-leashing her ringlets. Her pink blouse was one-third undone, a knotted leather cord nuzzled her clavicle, a camel-toned skirt clung to lithe hips, her slim hand wrapped around an earthy volume, which was, of course, her own.

Gordon stood before her for what seemed a long moment. Though he was not aware that he breathed, he assumed he must have, for soon, though it had been only suppertime when he fled Russet Avenue, Gordon found himself swept up in the morning rush hour.

Pouring down the stairs were thousands of 6 a.m. commuters. Where each normally held a newspaper, a *Sun* or *Globe* or *Star*, today they held only *Hello Twilight*. They descended like rain. Long lines of them pressed past Gordon, took their places on the platform, licking thumbs and turning pages that wept the thick unanimous whispering of *Chloe Gold, Chloe Gold, Chloe Gold*. Gordon let them carry him back down to the platform from which he had come — only a minute ago, a nighttime ago. The aquatic eyes of Poster Chloe followed him through the station, cold and green, from her seat above the stairs, her sunset head thrown back, a trace of a smile haunting her lips like the curling tail of a scorpion.

Northward Gordon rode, northward. The train doors had

slid open for him — and him alone, it seemed, the crowd on the platform too engrossed in their reading material to step forward and gain entrance before the doors-closing chime. *Tut-tut-tut-tut* Gordon's head went against an in-car poster. *Pantene: Collections that let you shine* had already been replaced by *Hello Twilight.* "Go Deeper," the poster hissed behind Gordon, its chrome frame pulling at his hairs, sexually, maliciously. "Go Deeper. Go Deeper. Go Deeper."

PART II

NOVEMBER

BEFORE TURNING TOWARD THE DOOR to her office, Lillian Payne pressed the button that closed the cupboard, and folding louvred panels clicked into place.

"Leave them," she commanded.

Her assistant stashed a stack of forms on the most available corner of the desk and hurried out again.

In two strides Lillian had retrieved them, wetted thumb, begun a page count, and simultaneously resituated herself before the louvred cupboard. When each page corner had passed by her forefinger and she had satisfied herself that the number of forms matched the number of employees she had hired in the past two months, she pressed the button that again slid open the immense folding doors. Behind them a wall-sized LCD screen contained numerous open windows, each an overhead view of a block of cubicles. Her gaze bounced between the monitor inside the cabinet and the names on the sheets before her.

Small, G., employee #1299, was typed on the top line of the first document.

Date of death:

Department:

Position:

Lillian removed a golf pencil from her pants pocket. In crisp letters she printed *September 22* beside *Date of death.* Mr. Small, G., was about to go from being a temp worker to a permanent one. Lillian shaded in the first few boxes without consulting the immense LCD screen where, in the top right-hand window labelled *Editorial 12-I,* the green-suited shape lurked. She examined the memo attached to his Employee Progress Report.

Memo from Head Office

To: Lillian Payne, Employee #10775

Re: Employee #1299

Please be advised that, as is often common among employees who come to us following an act of misadventure, our agents have noticed some amount of wandering on the part of employee #1299, also known as Small, Gordon, who was hired some time ago for your editorial department. Please be advised that he:

a)   did not report immediately to work post-interview ✓

b)   continues to leave the premises ✓

c)   continues to haunt the subway system ✓

d)   continues to haunt his previous home ✓

e) attempts to communicate or make contact with the living ✗

Reports indicate that this employee:

Visited his former residence on Russet Avenue. Saw his former possessions packed haphazardly. Acknowledged that his landlady was incapable of climbing up stairs or rearranging the furniture. Attempted to straighten the spines of boxed books. Noticed the hardwood floor had been faded by the sun. Paced about until he stood at the foot of the darker floorboards that defined where his bed had been situated. Turned his back to the space, lined his heels up against it, threw his arms wide, closed his eyes, and fell backwards.

Conclusion: The company believes the employee is under the impression that he still lives at this residence and that a new bed is to be delivered. He has journeyed there at least twice to sleep on his former lounge. Uses an old manuscript for a pillow.

Please be aware of these actions and, although it is possible they may be altogether ordinary, give this employee due scrutiny before advancing from temporary to permanent employ.

IT WAS A FORM LETTER with name, number, and specific details filled in. She had seen it dozens of times. Some employees had a more roving nature than others, some a more questioning one. It wasn't completely irregular for temps to get four checkmarks. She found they always settled down in their third and fourth months.

Lillian sorted through several reports. Acceptable reading time. Number of manuscripts completed per week: above average. Phone log/attendance: flawless. That was very good — if he had left the office as the report stated, he had managed to get back in time for working hours. Employees often missed days while they were still on temporary status. It was an adjustment period. She saw that he had signed on for Eden Eats, the online organic grocer owned by Heaven Books and operated by one of its sister companies. This was good also: it would keep him at Heaven. She nodded and observed this Mr. Small, G., on the flat-screen. He had complained to some of his co-workers about the reading material and had misfiled several of his time sheets and reports, but the filing had since become more regular.

The standard form for employee evaluations didn't leave room for a great deal of quibbling — or praise, for that matter. *Seems to be an ideal employee. Has the potential for long-term employ.* Lillian let her hand move past NO, MAYBE, and MOST LIKELY to check both YES boxes firmly. Lillian was forthright about checking off the boxes in a manner that would require the least follow-up from head office. If anyone had asked her, she would have answered honestly that she viewed her decisiveness as absolutely necessary for the efficiency of the company at large. Worried or weak evaluations only elicited premature investigation and subsequent paperwork. Both cost time and money. Lillian had stood by this belief for forty years without serious adverse consequence.

On the screen before her, Lillian spied her assistant about to knock on her door. Lillian closed the cupboard and let the folder on employee #1299 fall shut as the office door opened.

"I've just got word that Miss Chandler Goods has arrived," the assistant said. "She should be in the office bright and early on Friday."

"Ms., please," Lillian corrected. "This is a progressive company."

"Ms. Goods," the assistant parroted, "will be in the office on schedule."

7

AT NIGHT HEAVEN WAS QUIETER than any place Gordon had ever been. Inside that industrial subdivision, with its stretch of shipping depots, its Styrofoam-peanut makers, its factory outlet stores and big-box-style restaurants, the odd residential high-rise like a chancre amidst the naked hills, Gordon expected there to be some noise. Perhaps machinery or midnight whistles, the wizardry of bubble-pop manufacture, or printing presses rolling ink onto newsprint, cars revving or laughter ringing across parking lots, the noise of opened doors and video drone under the big, empty sky. Instead there was a thick wind and simple computer silence. The sound of noise with the human drained out of it, a sound made of nothing but the overhead lights.

Gordon had done what any reasonable man would do if his means of transportation were taken away by a mocking, movie-sized apparition of his ex — he had decided to spend the night at his place of work.

Full of good intentions, he'd actually worked through the

evening. It was eleven when Gordon pulled a hand across his eyes. The cubicle air wasn't dry, nor were his eyes strained from gazing at the outdated monitor, but he slumped back against his chair as if this were the case. There was a rumour that a window hadn't been opened at Heaven for more than twenty-nine years, and this had happened only when they were being replaced with new ones. Gordon had been reading for hours, following the onscreen text alongside the old-fashioned manu-scripts that the proofers pulled from an overflowing shelf down the hall, in the office of the executive who was never there but who was apparently their boss. Gordon recalled the references that had been made when he first interviewed with Lillian Payne: *Young international dynamo. Transferring over. Head-hunted. Worth the wait.* The head of Proofreading, Copy Editing, Substantive Editing, and Acquisitions — nine and a half floors of the Heaven building. The mysterious woman from whom Jon Manos took his directions.

When Gordon finished one manuscript, an eight-hour dedication, he went and immediately pulled out another. There were three piles, one extending up the set of shelves, the other two solid towers sitting in the middle of the floor and reaching respectively to Gordon's chest and to his waist. Proofers were supposed to pull from the tops of the piles, but as long as the manuscripts bore the same due date, a person could take any one he wanted without too much trouble. Gordon habitually scanned their titles, authors, and some-times first pages for goodies and baddies, though truthfully he had lost track of the difference after the first few weeks. Tonight he glanced anyway.

Gordon had developed a simple set of rules to live by at Heaven. Avoid manuscripts beginning with mild profanities such as "God!" "Damn!" "Double damn!" or worse, substitutes like "Horsefeathers!" "Granny's garters!" and "I don't give a flying fig!" It was almost certain that these books would be steeped in minor calamity and the characters likely to refer to each other's sexual parts as *bits, buns, rods, bosoms, honey-pots,* and *backsides.* Avoid manuscripts beginning with scenes of capture. If the female was endangered or imprisoned on the first page, a multitude of modern-day torn-bodice scenes would follow. The male character would almost always be irritatingly wealthy, in the end rewarding his prisoner of love with access to his mansion, his kingdom or princedom (kept secret until the climax), and his heart. Avoid books beginning in emergency rooms. Gordon would have welcomed the doctor–patient scenario, but most plots set in hospital revolved around doctor–nurse romance, and Heaven's female authors *did not* understand the notion of the naughty nurse. Heaven's nurses were healers, not feelers. They wore cardigans and ate eggs for supper. They were guaranteed to possess quaint ideals, live alone in large houses — just waiting to fill them with children — and of course waiting for the Mr. Right who could provide those children. *Dr.* Right, Gordon corrected himself as he flipped through one of these prescribed scripts.

He managed to secure what appeared to be a romantic jewel heist. Called *Night in Paradise, Paradise on Earth,* it was set in the tropics and included among its cast a Shakespeare-spouting parrot. It would not be hot; of this Gordon was almost certain. But the author was quoting Shakespeare where most quoted only Dr. Phil. Before midnight, however, the parrot had misquoted *A Midsummer Night's Dream*, a tangential character was speaking in bad patois, and out of habit and frustration Gordon was rubbing his eyes again. He decided to explore his own Night in Heaven.

HIS COLLEAGUES' DESKS were littered with personality, fragments of their daytime lives: Kinder toys, a plastic Madonna, clipped cartoon characters mounted on a cubicle wall, a coffee cup with an unwashed lipstick stain. What passed beneath his trailing fingers were used napkins, pocket change, the tabs of pop cans, eraser grit, the decapitated caps of pens, and scrawled sticky notes. What passed beneath his straying eyes were push-pins, collages of cheap sentiment, valentines and birthday cards stapled onto corkboard, magazine articles wrinkling at the corners, and paper dust, paper dust, paper dust.

Gordon discovered that the Designs were a vague presence even at night. A flock of them had lingered on in his periphery until eight or nine o'clock, and now two remained, popping silently in and out of their blue-walled world as Gordon edged around Floor Twelve, carrying his coffee mug as a kind of justification for his presence. A man in white pants and a black sweater glanced up at Gordon with some surprise, but then bent back again over his cutting board without worry. Gordon ventured down to the cafeteria and found a young cleaning woman wearing an immense set of headphones, an old transistor radio planted atop her cart of rags. On the same floor two duct men were peering up at the ceiling, several drop-tiles taken down and leaning against the thin side of the ladder. Beside them a large red case, presumably full of tools, perched on a counter. Gordon wondered what tools were used to keep a building of Heaven's size filtering and functioning, but the burlier of the two coveralls stopped speaking and gave him a pointed stare, as if waiting until Gordon had passed.

As Gordon wandered he found that the image of his wife still haunted him: Chloe standing on the front lawn of the house on Russet, *going deeper* with the manager of Champs as if she had met him before, had shared a personal or troubling experience already. Gordon pushed the mental picture of Chloe aside and attempted to ride the elevator up to Lillian Payne's floor, Seventy, but his pass card wouldn't take him there. He wound up down on Six, in the gym.

Gordon stripped down to his undershirt and boxer briefs. He hung his suit inside a vacant half-locker. It slumped upon the hook, green in the green locker. Gordon left it there alone and walked into the workout room.

On the conveyor of the treadmill, Gordon felt everything slide away from him. It was an amazing sensation. His head felt light and clear, his body surged forward without sweat. He ran into the night, seeming never to tire. He clocked over twenty miles without losing his breath. He ran from Russet Avenue, from the Dufferin Mall, from Grenwald, from Chloe, from Dr. Black and that still-remaining box of manuscripts, from himself. He ran toward a hundred heroines in a hundred new Heaven titles.

In the middle of the night Gordon eventually slowed to a walk and pressed Stop. He hit the weight bench. Though previously he had always felt as if his arms would tear out of their sockets if he continued very long, tonight there was an easy, dull rhythm to everything he did. The digital counter kept creeping its way to heavier decimals. Gordon attributed the lack of sensation to the adrenalin of the workout. Back in the men's change room, he gazed at himself in the mirror. His straw hair and usual dishwater complexion stared back. Something seemed odd . . . he wasn't sweating. Gordon placed a palm on the back of his neck — dry. Neither could he smell a thing. He headed for the showers anyway, convinced he had simply gone so far beyond stink that he had lost his senses. He let the water wash away the nothing, let his ears flood with the sigh of thrush faucet and the wind somewhere outside.

Again in his mind he saw Chloe cross the grass. Her sleeve fell back from her wrist, exposing the delicate copper hairs of her forearm.

"ARE YOU SUPPOSED TO BE HERE?" The security guard pivoted away from the portable television that sat inside his desk area. Gordon couldn't tear his eyes from the screen, where a familiar green scarf encased the ringlets that grew from a familiar head.

"Not really." Gordon flicked a finger in the direction of the tiny screen. "Can you turn it up?"

"Least you're honest." The security guard obliged and the volume jumped. "I shouldn't have let you in last night, then?"

"We're talking to Chloe Gold, author of *Goodbye to the Wind*, about her most recent opus, *Hello Twilight*." The host, a woman with a hairdo in six different shades of blond, held the book in her lap, one hand fluttering butterfly-like above its embossed cover. "Now, Chloe, I don't want to give too much away, but —"

The camera zoomed and lingered on Gordon's ex-wife's features. A tired, practised smile played across her lips. It seemed to him that she had aged even since yesterday, when he had stood not fifteen feet away from her.

"You didn't forget your cellphone, did you?" asked the guard.

Gordon batted his hand through the air as if he were swatting at flies.

The camera hadn't left Chloe. "Is it true that the book was inspired by the unexpected death of your ex-husband?" the host's disembodied voice queried.

Gordon wrapped a hand tight around the moulding that topped the guard's station.

Chloe gave a nod so tentative that Gordon at first did not want to believe she had.

"I know it's difficult," the host went on. As the camera returned to her, she bridged the divide to touch Chloe's hand briefly. "But try to tell us about that, if you can."

Without thinking, Gordon too reached out, past the lip of the security desk to the water bottle that sat there. It made its way to his mouth before he noticed the guard's fat glare.

"You mind?"

"Huh?"

The guard intercepted the bottle before Gordon could

drink again. He pried it from Gordon's hand and set it down on the desk. "Your cellphone —?"

"Never jumped on that trend." Gordon's eyes skipped between the guard, who was acting as if he was asking something serious, though Gordon could not deduce what could be serious about a cellphone, and Chloe, who after a moment of meandering, seemed to have redonned her publicity mask. It snapped eerily into place as she nodded with vigour.

"The excuse you gave me? To let you in after hours last night?" The guard raised his palm and waved thick fingers in front of Gordon's face.

"Right, yes, sorry." Gordon forced himself to focus on the guard's meaty face.

"I felt this incredible guilt at first, as though it was my fault —" said Chloe.

"Don't do it again."

"This book is more a reaction than a tribute though. . . . It just came from my guts. I'd abandoned another project I'd been struggling with for years, and then this one came so fast —"

"No," Gordon replied firmly before it appeared safe to turn his attention to the small screen again.

"Is she one of ours?"

"No," Gordon replied again. "Not any more," he added wistfully.

The guard's paw depressed the Off button, and Chloe became a dark reflection of the lobby. "Look," the security man growled. "Lots of folks got trouble. Not my business. But if you really can't go home at night, I suggest you try the concourse. *The Passage*," he emphasized when Gordon gave him a blank look. "Half the county's connected underground. Shop the friggin' night away. Sleep in your car, for all I care. Just don't wander my building. That's what I get paid for."

Gordon felt his head nodding on his neck, nearly as vigorously as TV-Chloe's had.

8

FOUR DAYS AND THREE MANUSCRIPTS LATER, it was raining. Sleety drops pelted the windows and reminded Gordon that outside Heaven dawn was arriving. His computer clock gave the time as 6 a.m. The security guard's rounds were minimal, Gordon had learned during that first stay-over, and he had managed to spend four full nights in Heaven. For four full days he had asked himself if he had misheard the interview with Chloe on the lobby television. Or had he gone mad? Either way, he rationalized, he should be more upset.

But *upset* wasn't the right word for any emotion that Gordon had experienced. He knew this. He hadn't cried since the day Chloe left him. That day he had sat at the top of the stairs in their rented row house. He hadn't been able to bear going down where he would see the living room half-empty. So he'd sat at the top, where he could see a six-foot patch of carpet at the bottom, and he'd stared at it — an orange and red striped rug, $49.99 from IKEA — for three hours. The stripes appeared and faded in varying stages of blurriness, breath cramping his lungs like that of an old man walking uphill. The quick leave. The slow wheeze. Finally he closed his eyes, and when he'd opened them the stripes were gone. Chloe had rolled them up and taken them while he sat there bawling. He had thought she would come up and say something to him before she left, something comforting, offer a last embrace. But, like now, he told himself, there was nothing to be said.

Through the Floor Twelve blinds the outside landscape looked like a grey, beat-up cat.

The previous evening before quitting time, Gordon had managed to slip up to the Internet Division to print out a blurb from an online book retailer: *A dead ex-husband. Unfinished love. Only Gold can pick up the pieces and show the absences in our lives with so much presence.* The publicity page Gordon printed out contained the publication date, the number of pages (548), the black-and-white author image with its eyes like thumbprints, and two-line reviews from all the bigs — *Publishers Weekly, New York Times, Chicago Review, Guardian, Globe and Mail.* The publication date especially gave Gordon pause. The online retailer had bungled the year. Or else, in only a couple of months, time had passed for Chloe, it seemed, at double, triple, quadruple speed. Since September, when Gordon had left Russet Avenue for Heaven, years seemed to have gone by. He recalled that first, endless transit ride.

Gordon stared down into the smudgy reproduction of Chloe's eyes. Every once in a while over the years, he'd asked himself if he still hated her. But when he found himself imagining *not* hating her, being happy for her success and her new life, it was akin to swiping too quickly with the razor at the spot on the very end of his chin. He pulled back from it, reeling.

Hate was a complex thing; it was like looking into a mirror. Chloe wasn't the same kind of writer that Gordon had been. She didn't look for approval. When they were living together, Gordon had always barked out lines like a performer of dinner theatre, needing to hear them aloud even as he wrote them, needing Chloe to hear them too. Although Chloe wrote quickly, frenetically, stacking up pages in the amount of time it took Gordon to write one or two, she tended to pull her manuscript pages from his hands, squeaking, "It's not ready!" and grabbing the pen and inking over the printed lines herself. The less she looked to him, the harder he argued against the very premise of her project, let alone individual lines of prose. They had once quarrelled for a whole hour about split infinitives. Or rather, he had quarrelled. It was unlike her not to argue back — she was supposed to; it was the part of her that was unquestionably Chloe — but she hadn't. And when she didn't, it lit something in him, and he raised his finger in the air like a Bible salesman calling on God to make his point. He had been right, he justified his actions now. Even with only two years on Chloe, he could see that her book was trite and juvenile, the work of a twenty-six-year-old.

Last night Gordon had automatically clicked on the space where the web site asked if he'd read the novel and would he like to rank it. He gave *Hello Twilight* a one-star rating. A moment later he'd realized that if its content was indeed based on him or his death, it was surely worthier of attention than her first novel. He clicked again for a five-star rating, but the site had recorded his first answer and would not let him vote twice.

He had then placed an order for *Hello Twilight* to be delivered to Heaven Books, 12205 Millcreek Industry Park, Floor Twelve, Attention: Gordon Small. In spite of a wallet teeming with pay stubs, he was skeptical about his credit — whether it would be good — but when he returned to his cubicle, he found he had received a confirmation e-mail.

Gordon took the publicity page for *Hello Twilight* and placed it very carefully inside a book that he believed no one would ever think to consult: an Australian dictionary of slang, between the entries *bull bar* and *bush oyster*. In turn he hid the book in the back of his bottommost drawer. It seemed safe beneath an atlas and a stack of magazine articles on grammar that had been photocopied and presented on a weekly basis, one by one, to Gordon and his co-workers by Manos, and occasionally by Erika — Manos's helper in spite of her own lack of understanding of the English language.

Behind the sound of rain Gordon could hear a shuffling coming from the editorial office at the end of the hall. He knew with certainty that there was only one other person left in the building. In the lobby eleven floors below slumped the security man, dozing. The Designs had all disappeared by midnight. Even the cleaners had cleared out. It was morning now, but early, too early for Bentley. Floor Twelve was filled with displaced air. Gordon sensed movement, though he saw no one.

Straightening up, he wound around the partitions toward the office where he usually picked up new manuscripts. In sock feet he padded softly through the hushed Heaven morning. Inside the office of the supervisor of their supervisor, Gordon spotted her. He saw her first through the glass panel to the left of the door, then from just inside as he entered quietly. He was stunned that the elevator doors could have opened — even once — to deposit her without him hearing.

The woman had wedged herself atop a stepstool and braced one knee precariously on a great stack of paper. Her backside was poised up, up, up on this pedestal of romance. It seemed to Gordon that the manuscripts he normally drew from in the second and third piles were rubber-banded into a kind of staircase leading up to her behind — which, he observed, was quite thrilling in shape. Encased in the ruby fabric of a tight-fitting skirt, the ass wiggled, engaged in the task before it. Ample in the best sense, the rear swayed as its owner retrieved and repiled, pitching manuscripts from the very farthest reaches of the first, never-ending shelf. Dangerous work. Over the woman's shoulder, pages came loose and cascaded to the floor as she discarded whole scripts, some furred with dust, pink work slips still attached to them, deadlines several years past.

The woman possessed legs the colour of milk, one extended and flexed tautly as she balanced, the other tucked underneath her, a black circular high heel spiking out from beneath the convex, complex ass. Floating to the floor, manuscript fragments:

"*I love you*,"
"*No, I you*,"
She wanted him to take her. Here, now . . .

Quickly and completely . . .
He inhaled sharply . . .

Gordon realized he too must have gasped, because the next moment, the woman turned. Her heel sought a foothold where there was none. With the twist and the woman's shock at seeing him, the stack of manuscripts beneath her loosened. Gordon watched: sixty-nine rubber bands snapped simultaneously and the next two weeks of Heaven work leaned, Tower of Pisa–like, and lurched into one mess of romance. Authors kaleidoscoped into one another. Sex occurred with first meetings, heroines landed atop heroines, marriages got parked beside mid-story faux breakups that would now find no resolution. French kisses occurred in front of Grandma. The roping of rodeo horses was tied to bedroom scenes in instant bondage sessions. The candles in a seventeenth-century chandelier in Italy were set ablaze and heaved into the air as a nineteen-year-old in present-day Brooklyn removed her brassiere for the very first time before a companion.

"Oh!" the woman exclaimed, her eyes wide. Arms whirled, legs split, spike heels kicked.

The woman landed indelicately across Gordon's crotch, one leg over each of his shoulders, panties within view, his own back end planted perfectly atop the meshed manuscripts of *Sweet Surrender* and *Overtaken by Passion*. A hurricane of pages hurtled over their heads, smashed down around them.

"This is *no* way to meet," the woman said without a hint of sarcasm, her lips just inches from his, their eyes locked.

"Gordon Small, proofreader, full-time," Gordon said, proud to be able to swear off temp status. He offered her his hand after extracting it from beneath a heap of *Love on the Range*.

She shook it as politely as possible under the circumstances. "Chandler Goods, head of Editorial, just relocated from Heaven Paris."

"My . . . boss?"

"Yes, I —" She glanced down at the crotch of her underpants, suddenly realizing they were so present.

Before Chandler Goods could move and before Gordon had thought about it much, he leaned forward and sealed his lips to hers. He had kissed a couple of women since Chloe — bungled set-ups or pickups that had ended abruptly after he'd lunged forward and planted a juicy one — but it had been a long time. Flicking his tongue between Chandler's teeth, he felt no resistance, and deepened the kiss. Sitting atop the trembling loins of a thousand imaginary virgins and suitors, she tasted like rose petals and paper dust — mostly the latter. There wasn't the awesome wetness he remembered from long-ago kisses.

Pulling back for a second, he muttered, "It's almost the same."

"What —?"

His mouth engulfed hers again, as if it were a cheese puff or a sausage roll offered up in a grocery aisle taste test. For the first time since Gordon had come to Heaven, he thought he felt his heart kick distinctly, twice, in his chest: *Chand-ler*. He had definitely gone nuts, he decided in the middle of the second kiss.

Chandler Goods seemed to come to her senses, separating her bee-stung lips from his and extracting herself from his rigor mortis lap.

"Who did you say you were?"

She backed slowly off Gordon. She pressed her fingertips to her temple and turned on her heel toward the window, where the bleary day was quickly breaking. When she spoke again, her voice trembled. The words came out fast and furious. "It's not even seven o'clock. My intention was to get a jump on all this." She gestured at the dishevelled manuscripts cascading out from where Gordon sat. "Not to get jumped." The words caught in her throat. "You come in here, spy on me and — with absolutely no provocation . . . no, really, *none* whatsoever — molest me." She turned and bent, jammed a finger in Gordon's chest. "Who do you think you are?"

MUCH LATER THAT DAY, Gordon leaned forward, hooked his lips with index fingers, and ejected tongue from mouth so that it stuck straight out. In the Floor Six locker room mirror, he watched his image do the same. He plunged forward recklessly, let his tongue make contact with the glass, but when he retracted it, it left no saliva. Neither did the mirror fog when he attempted an impromptu zerbert, buzzing his lips against its silver surface.

He had spent several hours checking himself, but every hair was as he remembered it. Loosely muscled arms, like white gym-shoe laces, dangled from his shoulders. His pale, tufted gut — which had always varied between gaunt and paunchy depending upon where he was eating — was, to Gordon's delight, on the thin side. Gordon's body was, quite simply, as *his* as he had ever known it — though it had ceased to digest or secrete. Gordon recognized that when he had been eating during those first weeks at Heaven, it must have been out of habit, for now he had gone five days without food and had not experienced one pang of hunger or thirst. Habit was psychology. Habituation, a simple form of learning, the adoption of repeated patterns of behaviour. Children had habits. Animals had habits. *Even the insane, especially the insane, have habits they do not stray from,* Gordon told himself. It was habit too for the mind to conjure the smells and tastes it wanted to remember, the smells and tastes it associated with the names or shapes of things.

His skin did seem remarkably translucent above the three-day beard that lent him the air of a yellow Easter rabbit. "You should stand a little closer to a razor, son," the Whoopsy's franchise owner had perpetually told him. In its usual fashion, Gordon's blond-brown hair was combed half over his forehead to hide the recession and shagged out behind his ears. His lips were still full, red and rubbery, not unlike those candied wax lips he had bought as a child from a bin for a quarter, chewed on, and then spat out. His eyes were like dark cracked marbles, but if they hinted at his mortality he suspected it was no more than they had during his life. His nose still hung with the bravado of a large appendage, and as for that other appendage, it appeared to function as well as any of those belonging to the heroes in Heaven's books — it was serviceable, though he did not seem to be able to achieve a medical definition of release.

When he had redonned his green suit, Gordon flipped off the change-room light and exited the gym, walking through an expanse of black. The weight machines in one corner looked like a small factory of stacks and scaffolding against the light thrown up from the street lamps below the window. "Hello, twilight," he said as he crossed the floor. Outside the glass the concrete cul-de-sac that stretched away from the building looked dark and damp. He attempted to whistle, but found that he could not draw a breath that wasn't attached to a word.

9

"SHOULD BE HERE BY NOW." Daves peered earnestly out the glass doors.

Gordon paced back and forth in the lobby with him under the peevish gaze of the security guard.

"Man, this is *torture*. I swear to you, this happens with delivery every time I'm working late," Daves muttered, checking his watch.

"Every time?"

"Sure." Daves bounced back and forth on the great rubber soles of his hiking shoes. "I can taste the pepperoni already. An hour, an hour and it should be free."

"Don't you think it's a little weird, Daves, that 2-4-1 Pizza can't find a building this size? With so many people who work here, there must be tons of takeout."

Outside the doors, sunset was bubbling on the grey horizon like a bright, thick sauce just about to burn itself onto the bottom of a pan. It was almost six, and the tower rose above them. Most people were already gone or sweeping final files into drawers.

"Wouldn't they call if they couldn't find it?" Gordon suggested smoothly. He wondered if Daves suspected what he, Gordon, increasingly thought might be true about the state of things in Heaven. Tonight, from Gordon's side of things, pizza was not pizza. Pizza was hypothesis. "Maybe I should head back up and see if there's a message."

"Don't tell me you haven't noticed," Daves said, his eyes never leaving the cul-de-sac in front of Heaven.

The hairs on Gordon's forearms rose like a row of soldiers.

"How long have you been here?" Daves scoffed, turning for just a second from the glass doors. "The phones." He made a punctuation sign with his eyes, waiting for Gordon to get it.

Gordon fiddled in his jacket pocket for the quarter that had crept its way into the lining, though the suit jacket, however wrinkled, remained too new for this to have happened. It was his only way to stall, to keep the look on his face from betraying his disappointment with Daves. Something about the phones was all Daves had to tell him?

"Have you ever heard them ring?" Daves challenged.

Gordon gave up on the invisible coin. "People are always on them —" he began.

"Calling *out*."

They both stared out the doors. The light from the sunset painted them, filtered past their two shapes into the dulling foyer.

"I'm sure I have," Gordon insisted.

"Very, very, very occasionally," Daves confirmed. "It's

unnerving, is what it is — an office building with no ringing. It's just not right. I haven't heard an outside call since I got here," he declared, "and that's a helluva lot longer than you've been here."

In spite of himself, Gordon liked the way this kid was always reminding him of his place.

"There are calls within the building, see, from one extension to another. But you have to be from a different department or you'll go direct to voice mail. See, I can call *you* direct, because I'm in Layout, but you can't call Jill without it hitting her machine, because you're both Proofreading. The idea is that cross-department calls are likely to be more important than interdepartment ones, which are often personal. Ringing through to the message system," Daves explained, "means our work isn't interrupted. You can call out or you can pick up your messages, but you never get the ring. And outside calls? Forget it. The whole life of Heaven revolves around production. High wages are the instrument used to select and maintain in stability a skilled labour force suited to the system of production and work."

"What? Is that Gramsci?"

"So the phones don't ring: coercion outweighs consent." Brow furrowed, eyes still trained on the distance, Daves detailed his argument, holding up fingers. "One: work lacks intellectual content."

Gordon nodded; that it did.

"Two: mechanization. Three: routinization and simplification of tasks. What's your job?"

"I — I read."

"Anything else?"

"No. But —"

"Four: fragmentation. Oh sure, you can pick up the books off the shelf when they're done, but it's not like you were there for the cover's *fine* photo shoot, were you? Ever meet any of our randy authors?"

Gordon shuddered at the thought. "Maybe we should phone again."

"Our product is lust and our activity is up. A bona fide industrial plant stands above you, my friend," Daves continued cheerfully. "The wheels of romance turn with Fordism."

"I thought you really liked your job."

Daves nodded as if he did, but what he said was, "Bottom line: work speeds up."

Suddenly "The Camptown Races" sounded across the lobby. Daves dug in his pocket and pulled out a pulsing, cantering cellphone. It shone in the last light. "Why do you think I always keep this on me?" he boasted to Gordon's shocked expression. "Y'ello!" Daves barked into its silver mouth. "Yep, that's us. . . . Yep, we're right here at the door. . . . I don't see your car. Which door you at?" Daves' face clouded and he craned against the glass. "Yeah . . . that's right, that's right, but — but where *are* you?"

Daves wrapped his hand around the door handle. "We gotta go outside," he said around the phone, "flag 'em down. He says he's on Millcreek, but he must be circling in the visitors' parking lot."

Gordon peered past Daves. There was the phone call, but no delivery car was to be seen. He didn't remember crossing a visitors' parking lot when he'd come for his interview. Daves was wrong; the car simply wasn't there.

Daves pulled on Heaven's door handle, but it didn't budge. The security light on the side turned orange.

Security Bear was instantly beside them, all stubble and heft. He shook his scratchy hair back from his scratchy face and fixed them with a stare that said *Forget it*. "This time a day I have to swipe it, then sign you back in. You *know* I'm not authorized to do that after hours 'less you got a overtime pass."

"We just want the delivery. You want a slice? Hell, have half the pizza," Daves offered.

"Love to." Security Guy didn't move. "But you got rules, I got rules, we all got rules — whatcha gonna do?"

"I don't have to be here," Daves snapped.

Security just looked back at him.

Daves let his lips sputter. "Come on!" he demanded of the guard.

When Security didn't move, Daves jabbed his head to one side like Grenwald. To Gordon he mumbled, "Damn, we're never gonna get that extra-large." Disgusted, he clicked off the phone and tucked it under his shirttail. He leaned against the glass with a last withering look outside. "And I thought that Madam Chow's was incompetent. Hell, out here everyone's incompetent. I can't stand it, I gotta smoke."

It was the first time Daves had mentioned his vice. He and Gordon headed behind the elevator, back past the glowing women's-bathroom hallway. Gordon followed Daves out a magenta door. Beyond was the darkening glass of an exit. They wound up in a courtyard in the centre of Heaven. The building was literally all around them. Seventy floors above them hovered a thirty-by-thirty-foot square of sky, complete with the last pale streaks of a late November sundown. There was no wind in this vertical tunnel, but the cold hit Gordon like a shock, like a snowball, like something hard, joyous, and straight out of his youth. They were actually outside. The air was crisp as an ice puddle, yet Gordon couldn't see their breath. The sky was far away, but so real, stoic, and grand that it reminded Gordon of a lion in a zoo. He stood staring up into it, almost welling up, nostalgic for sky.

Next to him Daves removed a crumpled pack of smokes from his flannel pocket. The outdated packaging caught Gordon's eye. Daves held it out to him.

"Sure." Between Gordon's fingers the cigarette felt slim and satisfying. He leaned into the flame but found he didn't have the breath to drag back on it. Daves flipped his Zippo closed. As old as the packaging was, the tobacco didn't taste stale. Gordon held the cigarette close to his mouth and let the smoke drift lazily and of its own accord over his lips. He could still taste, and the taste was like metal and wood, a memory of stealing away outdoors, adolescence.

He repeated what Daves had said in the foyer. "'They're all incompetent out here.' Where do you live, Daves?" Would Daves go as foggy on the question as Georgianne Bitz had the time Gordon pressed her for directions to Job City?

Daves attempted a smoke ring but the smoke just wafted out of him, and immediately afterward he looked self-conscious — which Gordon hadn't thought possible — and wandered around the courtyard with the cigarette clamped between his lips, hands in his pockets. "Thornhill," Daves said, coming back around.

"You like it?"

He shrugged. "I was born there."

Gordon flicked the ash amateurishly. He baited Daves. "How much do these set you back a week?"

"You don't smoke, huh?"

Gordon shook his head, kept staring at the sky way up above them. Seen through a window, the sky could just as well be made of paper, but this, Gordon had to admit, smelled like snow, like earth.

Daves rattled off the price of his smokes, and Gordon raised his eyebrows. He held out the cigarette briefly and peered at it as if it could talk, tell him something different. "That's all?"

Daves didn't miss a beat. "Yep, but I don't smoke much, you know. Not like those guys who rip through a pack a day or something. I can't even tell you how long I been on this same one. I mean, you gotta be careful. It'll kill you."

"Sure ... sure ..."

"Poison of the working class, the things we can afford."

Gordon wondered if Daves' father had been a foreman and he couldn't shake the blue-collar notion — or if he was simply young enough still to be enthralled by the idea of being down-at-heel. "I was never much of a smoker," Gordon said, lurching into the past tense without thinking about how Daves would interpret it. "Not this stuff anyway. It is focusing, though." Gordon held the butt in his lips and inhaled as best he could, which was more like letting the smoke float across his mouth.

"Ever smoke outside the other doors? That would be nicer, with people going in and out." But it wasn't the view that Gordon cared about; after the pizza fiasco, he wondered whether anyone came or went through the grand double doors besides new interviewees.

The courtyard was dark and getting darker. The cigarette ends didn't glow when they sucked, but Daves didn't notice.

"Yeah, well, like everything good, there's rules against it." Smirking, Daves held up so-scared hands. "Looks bad. Company image. God forbid the individual should exist." He grinned when he said this. He looked good, Gordon reflected, for a guy who'd been dead five years or more, judging by the price and the look of his smokes.

They shared a laugh and butted out.

"Double cheese," Daves marvelled on the way back in, shaking his head wistfully.

10

CHANDLER GOODS'S E-MAILS were always paired with subject lines that would have set Gordon's pulse racing, if he'd had one. Unfortunately the messages seldom lived up to the promise.

"Your male opinion" meant she wanted to know if he had noticed Carma's skirt, and whether she should get one. "Thinking of you" meant she had straightened out his productivity report with Manos. "Speaking of romance" meant she could not concentrate at all on the business of romance publishing because Titus Bentley was distracting her. She believed Titus had power issues that were "affecting the Floor Twelve vibe." The subject line "A proposal" meant she needed a coffee break — could she steal Gordon for ten minutes of accompaniment?

Gordon was in no position to refuse. He was a lowly proofreader, at the very bottom of Chandler's department. She could have adopted a comrade from Copy Editing, Substantive, anywhere really. His best guess as to how he had happened to fill the position of Chandler's confidant was his convenient location on her floor, combined with the fact that he seldom spoke. He refrained from writing back that, now that he noticed it, Carma had been wearing the same skirt for three months, likely three years; that Titus *definitely* affected the Floor Twelve vibe, and that the anxiety he emitted was a symptom of his necrosis. Gordon also refrained from letting on that coffee had become his greatest joy and sorrow.

"Gord, what's up? It's *Friday*," Chandler commented on his sour expression, breezing into the kitchen as if she had no intention of being there. She walked in fast yet hesitant, the way she always did. *In a hurry*, her body said, but also, *Just passing through.* This struck Gordon as incredibly cute, since Chandler was only about five feet four in her heels. She had almost made her way out of the kitchen when she stopped at the doorway and doubled back, won over by the mocha scent. As usual she didn't have her cup with her. She scrounged around the back of cupboards, which were too high for her to see. As she was going through her cup-at-the-back-of-the-cupboard routine, he found himself once again swept into an unexpected appointment with her rear end. Titus Bentley, as well as a number of men from Design, sat at the table in the middle of the room, silently sipping from their own fully possessed coffee mugs, each head tipped to a forty-five-degree angle, parallel to Ms. Goods's goods. Bentley's lewd mouth seemed to tear his entire face.

Chandler's hands crept blindly across an empty shelf above her head. Her teeth stapled her bottom lip. One knee leaned against the cupboards for leverage, the other foot off the floor.

The loose ruffles of her short sleeves fell back to her shoulders, and the muscles bunched beneath them. All of her streamed upward with exertion, including her breasts. Even her eyebrows arched, a bank of effort appearing across her forehead. She glanced in Gordon's direction, then her gaze flew back to the shelf above her.

Gordon walked over to the gathering of gawkers. He kicked the table's leg. Coffee cups splashed black liquid over the edges. The men jolted, unfroze. Gordon stepped over and produced a cup for Chandler — the one he had brought in with him. After a quick rinse, he handed it over. She blushed, the flush extending across her face and into the cleft of her blouse. "Thank you," she said, her shoulders falling as if they understood better than her brain the scene that had just played out behind her.

"I don't know why I do that," Chandler said, pointing to the shelf, herself, the shelf, her eyes doing an embarrassed dance between the two. "But that's me." She peered at the straps around her ankles that fastened to curved black heels. "And these aren't getting any taller." She filled Gordon's mug, double-double, and they walked back to her office. "I'm developing a very serious relationship with that shelf," she yammered. "That third shelf and I." She crossed two fingers over each other.

"Oh, I'm sure you say that about all the shelves," Gordon quipped, and without expressly being asked, he found himself once again inside Chandler's shimmering office. She went through helter-skelter motions of cleaning up without actually seeming to rearrange any of the piles. Gordon inwardly acknowledged the effort as a sign of her self-consciousness.

She liked him. He had saved her. She was drinking from his mug. It was as easy as something written on paper.

When his hands were empty, Gordon knew, he had his own nervous habit of digging through his pockets for lint, or that imaginary coin. With his mug cradled firmly in her palm, he had nothing to hide behind. So he reached out decisively and plucked a handful of unsharpened pencils from a stout holder of whorled pink glass. He set about the task of sharpening them with a metal wedge. Small pulpy flowers bloomed into one palm as he turned the yellow wood round and round.

"Making yourself useful? Careful, I could get used to having an assistant."

"A male assistant in particular?"

"Oh, I'm really not particular," she said, missing — or ignoring — his invitation entirely.

What good was the afterlife if you were less of a Casanova in it than in real life? Gordon asked himself. Did one really have to be oneself, even here?

Chandler tossed her hair and set the steaming mug down on the desk, both her hands wrapped around it as if for warmth, though one thing Gordon had noticed long ago was the building's temperature; even as fall had turned to winter, Heaven seemed to have a flawless thermostat. It was unlike any place Gordon had ever been: work, school, libraries, restaurants, waiting rooms.

"Is it colder here than in France?" he asked.

"Well, France is north of here, of course. But dampness, crispness — there are different kinds of cold, I'd say. France is no England, for instance. But, you know," she continued, as if the thought were occurring to her only as she spoke, "I haven't had to change my wardrobe. When I left I just assumed I'd buy anything I needed when I got here, but . . . who has time, and I haven't really found it necessary. I can't complain, for a move across an ocean." She sank into the coffee steam, getting down level with the cup, her chin nearly on her elbow upon the desk. "You know what I do miss?"

He watched as she eyed the cup with melancholy. "Café au lait?"

"The sunlight. Paris sunlight is just different."

Gordon crumbled three pencils' worth of trimmings into the wastebasket. As they fell, he felt his thumb and ring finger rub together, and just for a second he felt the familiar absence of Chloe's ring, which was still inside a velvet golf-ball-sized box beneath the briefs with the waistband half torn away in the top drawer of the dresser in the upstairs bedroom on Russet Avenue. At least, it *had* been there, he reminded himself. "How can sunshine be different?"

"Oh, you wouldn't say that if you'd ever been to Indiana. The light there is like water leaking out of a cracked glass."

"What does Indiana have to do with Paris?"

Chandler took a long gulp from Gordon's coffee mug, as if swallowing her own fear. "It's where I'm from."

The question in Gordon's mind was: how had Chandler got to Heaven? The question he put forth was: how had she got to Paris?

The way that Chandler explained it, life for her had begun in the outlying farm areas around Indianapolis. "The Crossroads of America" was her town's grand motto, though to apply it to the rural area where the Goods family resided was munificent. Chandler described herself as one of those eager, over-anxious children, the kind who were constantly spinning in circles or turning the tiniest problems over and over in their minds in order to avoid running about and playing with the sockets. By sixteen, in a whirl of summer romance, she'd gone and got her heart broken worse than one might think imaginable, considering she'd never actually kissed the boy himself — or any boy, for that matter. Though she'd always had difficulty with attendance at school, her solution to heart-break was to inhale the smell of ink from every page of every textbook within the very first month of junior year. She soon skipped ahead, progressing straight to senior. If it was a jail-break to get out of Indianapolis, Chandler had decided to go the whole nine yards, treating the state and all its outlying crossroads like San Quentin. Though she applied to top schools across the country for scholarships and bursaries, her true goal was to get off the continent. A convenient, unknown uncle in Scotland emerged at that point in the story, and a letter.

Gordon paused in his listening to imagine the rudimentary nature of the letter, the penmanship of one Chandler Goods, age sixteen, in blue felt-tip on airmail paper thinner than the Goods' household TP, the flag — like one of surrender — on the three-quarter-inch stamp waving yet immobile as Chandler's then-lineless hands clutched the envelope tightly. He imagined her blowing on it for luck and dropping it finally into the dark of the box on the block where she had lived her whole life, a series of unknown sacks and baggage compart-ments awaiting it.

The uncle responded, also in letter form, approximately thirty days later, enclosing the most beautiful photograph Chandler had ever seen: the countryside of his "modest, but by all means serviceable estate."

Gordon had an uncanny feeling that he had heard this story before, but he said nothing.

Though her parents had protested her choice, Chandler had believed their protective instincts were motivated by their desire to keep her harnessed to a life of mediocrity. And so she ascended, hovering over the Atlantic, heart buoyed by girlish dreams — all of which would be dashed in the days to come.

An uncle with no aptitude for pleasantries retrieved her from the airport and drove her farther and farther from civilization, to his indeed "modest but serviceable" estate, the only benefit of which was the view of the neighbours' far more lovely, sprawling, and completely unpopulated properties. With a shock Chandler recognized these from the photograph she had kept tacked above her desk in Indiana. She found herself cloistered in a small stone cottage. It had no telephone and few modern conveniences, and the exterior resembled a crumbling, forgotten prison. The romantic in Chandler vowed to make the best of her situation, and she spent her first few hours writing postcards announcing her arrival, and even an original poem on the first page of a shiny hard-backed journal she had bought for the purpose of recording her new life.

The entries that followed were streaked with tears, and Gordon sat aghast as Chandler recounted in detail her uncle's demonic behaviour, which began that very night with an unhealthy monitoring of her personal habits and led in the days to come to intercepting her outgoing and incoming mail (from her university applications to her pleas to her parents for plane fare), building to a nightly imposition of his basest desires upon her unsuspecting, often sleeping, corpus. He had horrid whiskers, and fouler breath. Though he had lost one hand years before, he took particular delight in attempting to stimulate her with his sinister clamps, stroking her feminine flesh with his unfeeling steel, and — on those days when he feared she might flee from his advances — wielded his medieval hook like a weapon, holding it to her throat as she struggled against him.

Gordon attempted to interrupt Chandler at this uncomfortable point to warn her that he was sure he had read just such a thing in a Heaven title the previous week, but she patted his hand on the third word out of his mouth — as if he were attempting to console her — and rushed on.

She had fought her uncle always, though he continued to tell her how much sweeter their love would be if she would only give in to what he knew was her heart's true desire. He took to referring to her as his "American mail-order," and ordered her about the isolated garden by the name Bride. When she found the marriage licence among his papers, her forged signature and the deadline of their pending appointment led her to grasp the direness of her situation. She would need to do more than merely survive his abuse; she would need to escape now or perish in what would become a lifetime of sexual submission and servitude, a regulated schedule of eternal misery.

By the time Chandler arrived at this juncture in her story, ten proofreaders had trooped through to pick up twelve new manuscripts (two of the same faces twice) and Gordon had cultivated a garden of pencil shavings that topped the wastebasket, threatening to drop sooty petals to the floor. Most of Chandler's pencils were now nubs. At this vital point Chandler became so ambiguous about her "escape" from the situation that Gordon began to suspect that she had resorted to the rope or the razor.

"Maybe life is just a series of increasingly bizarre escapes," he interjected, in an attempt to comfort and also to prompt. A paternal desire overcame him, to reach out and stroke her elbow or her hair, but he tamped it down.

Chandler smiled that self-deprecating smile, the one that emphasized not only her dimple but the faint lines around her mouth as well. No matter how long she had lived under the malicious thumb of her uncle — assuming there even was an uncle — she could not have lived there as many years as fell between seventeen and thirty. The skin around her eyes was still lusciously unyielding, but her mouth was more pliant: she was no child.

Gordon questioned her as congenially as one can when inquiring into absconding from rapist relatives. He quickly determined that, in spite of what it said on her business card, Ms. Chandler Goods had never been to Paris — at least, she had not actually wandered its streets.

Rather, her knowledge was rooted in the vocabulary of a would-be tourist, book learning melded with fantasy gleaned from movies and photographs — or perhaps, it occurred to Gordon, in the vocabulary of someone stationed just slightly above the city, viewing it from an unchanging position, a permanent window. In Chandler's Paris there were no beggars, no dog droppings, no confused tangle of metro lines, none of the fine filth that covered the city and crept its way under Gordon's nails and even into his nostrils, darkening his phlegm when he spat, during the few days he had spent there while still a student, backpacking around Versailles, the Louvre, the Sorbonne, Sacré Coeur in Montmartre, and, of course, the Lizard King's grave. Chandler's apartment had no neighbourhood, or if it did, it was a strange patch of land able to levitate and switch from Left to Right Bank at will; she had no transit route to work and no friends outside the office; she had never been to a nightclub; she did not know the number of francs for a Coca-Cola or a *bouteille de vin*, nor the name of the *boulangerie* where she bought her *petit déjeuner*. The only thing she seemed able to detail with any accuracy was the work she did. And even that, strangely, was in English, as though, in spite of the prevalence of French names, Chandler's entire department was a flock of expats.

Whether she noticed his sudden spike in curiosity or not, Chandler meandered right back around to Paris sunshine, placing her head on her palm with a sigh. "It's like a net thrown over the sky to try to catch the clouds. In the morning the sky was always white along the bottom, and overhead a pale '70s blue . . . like my mother's eyeshadow."

"How . . ." Gordon tossed a handful of shavings — and an entire pencil nub along with them — into the trash. "How could you give two poops about sunshine after everything you went through?" Two things occurred to him even as the question escaped. The first was that he had just asked about something he didn't even believe. The second was that he had quite naturally reached for the phrase "two poops" instead of the beloved four-letter version he had favoured when he worked at the mall.

Chandler leaned her head into her hand like a twelve-year-old. She peered at his mug, now empty, as she hooked a pinky finger through its handle and dangled it, letting it swing, her eyes following the impromptu pendulum. "Everywhere you go, Gordon . . . everywhere—" She glanced past the mug to him as if offering it back. "You have to find something . . . at least one thing to love."

He reached out and took the mug carefully from her fingers, which were cool to the touch. The phrase "the cool hand of a girl" came to his mind, but he banished it with a half-hearted smile.

NOW THAT HE WAS CERTAIN he was dead, Gordon was gripped by thorough disappointment. He expected to remember important things about his living years — the life-altering moments. But what he remembered were mundane, passing-time errands and meandering. In fact, what he remembered most clearly was contemplating buying a carry-on for a vacation he never wound up taking. The carry-on had thick black straps and leather on the handles, a thick silver zipper and a leather logo patch — and the saleswoman, name-tagged Anita, had smiled in a super-genuine way. He remembered standing in the store with a riot in his stomach, wondering if he should shell out the seventy bucks so she could make her commission, deciding in the end to postpone it for the express purpose of a return trip to the store and a future conversation. For weeks Gordon had walked by, peripherally obsessed, attempting to monitor Anita's shifts so he could ask her out, but in the end never going back and doing it, and never buying the carry-on either.

Prior to working for Heaven Books, his life for many years had been an urban mall. His memories were Freshly Squeezed, Bubble Tease, Jimmy the Greek, Roasty Jack, New York Fries, Made in Japan, Bagel Stop, Cinnabon, Carlton Cards, Deco Home, Payless, Radio Shack, Island Inkjet, HMV. The cherry rosettes of photograph-perfect ice cream cups were frequently replaced by seasonal promotions tied in with children's films Gordon knew about but hadn't seen. *Surf's Up! Fruit Blast! Splish Splash! Penguin Swirl!*

Now when Gordon tried to remember the important things — like his wedding to Chloe, or even their wedding *night* — it was like holding one shoe in his hand, and leaning over, peering under beds for the other. The memories were cobwebbed, dark. But the temperamental price gun from Whoopsy's Gags 'N Gifts still jammed in Gordon's hands, and he could still visualize the cartoon faces on the latest batch of *Simpsons* T-shirts. SpongeBob SquarePants Forever Bubbles key chains retailed for $4.75. His inner retail voice trumpeted: *Add that to the movie poster for $7.99 and you've just bought a fabulous birthday present for LESS than $15.00 — with tax!* Cultural detritus floated up at him, dreamlike. He recalled bikini-girl beer holders, classic horror-movie calendars, and in the fish bowls that lined the counter, rock 'n' roll buttons, rubber lizards, dice with sexual commands printed on their sides, innovatively shaped pencil toppers, and light-up gel pens. *I know you'll be happy with your purchase. Thank you for shopping at Whoopsy's.* There were bug boxes with magnifying lids, perfect for catching insects in, and Gordon had pocketed one imme- diately and used it to carry his magic pills. The sound the Vivatex tablets had made, the first few days he'd carried them like this, was like a tiny maraca teeming with beans. To the left of his heart, where he kept the pills even now, inside his shirt pocket, invisible, the eraser-sized see-through box rattled with the pleasure of his pain. As white as Chloe's birth control pills, they had become his own kind of control. Gordon remem- bered ordering tubs of French fries and waiting.

A FEW DAYS LATER, when Gordon next joined Chandler in her office, her confessions had evaporated. It did not take long for Gordon to realize that Chandler's confidences were about as deep as her e-mails: banged out in a frenzy and sent off with no forethought, no reread, no fear about the impression she was making nor any hope of answer. This time she went into a two- hour inventory of the workforce she had left behind in Paris.

"Daniel was known for his little dog, and photographs of little dogs, and conversations full of little dogs; Lizette for top buttons undone; Laurent for middle buttons undone; Eduard for worshipping the Tour de France, for slinking in and out of rooms silently, his body sleek as a bicycle."

At the end of her prattle, seemingly without any prompt, Chandler dug under a stack of folders and came out with a stiff cardboard package, which she handed him. *Gordon Small, Heaven*, it said on the rectangular label.

"For you?" she asked with a hint of suspicion, even though the bookseller's logo was prominently printed in the return address corner.

Gordon nodded, and without another word he took it away. As he walked he let his hands slip up and down as if weighing something, enjoying the shape the cardboard made against his skin. It didn't feel nearly as heavy as he had expected it to.

In his cubicle he tore his finger open on the staple. He put it in his mouth and sucked, though there was no blood, and no saliva with which to suck. As the cardboard gates opened he saw that the cover was not the blue-green twilit expanse he had anticipated. The book was a mottled wine colour, and the adorning name did not belong to Gordon's ex-wife. Half in roman type and half in script, the title declared: *The Purpose-Driven Life*. Gordon dropped the book and its packaging abruptly on the desk and sat staring at it.

A moment later, Chandler e-mailed. Her subject taunted: "Is it good?" The body of her message read: *What did you get?*

Gordon used one finger to push *The Purpose-Driven Life* inch by inch across the surface of his desk. It hung half on and half off, then fell with a wallop into his garbage basket.

The wrong thing, he wrote.

11

GORDON GLANCED UP to see if anyone was nearby before he pulled the tabs from his desk drawer and tore the mailing sticker clear. He smoothed it onto his envelope. Over the past two weeks, as he had come to terms with the discovery of his own demise, Gordon had penned and stamped three submissions to literary magazines — two stories and a selection of five poems — all about his relationship with Chloe Gold. He felt a strange sense of freedom. Gordon Small had gone beyond the grave, and anything he wrote now, regardless of its invective, no one could hold against him. He had located the postage machine in Manos's cubicle one night recently and printed off a stack of tickets to ride. He considered each submission a test. Not of his own abilities, but of their ability to travel outside of Heaven. He tapped the current envelope against his lips in a silent goodbye-and-good-luck.

Gordon's nights now heaved with punctuation, but not the mere additives of commas and colons that he salt-sprinkled into the pulp as it passed by him during the day. If one were to label the cubicles like booths in a restaurant, Gordon's would be the one hundred and thirty-third, the very last fuzzy pink booth. It was there, sometime past midnight, after Security's rounds, that Gordon began his real work, with a black ball-point pen clenched between back molars. *What I have been given here at Heaven is truly a gift*, Gordon keyed. *Endless hours, infinite light, paper supplies, envelopes, free postage.*

Now, envelope in hand, Gordon made a daytime trip up to the Heaven Web on Floor Fifty-Eight, where he took a whirl on Ivy's computer, 411ing addresses. Soon Gordon's borrowed rose-brown envelopes had dropped with a delicious *snap* into the outbox. Monitoring the outbox, however, proved more difficult than Gordon had assumed.

"When will they pick this up?" he asked Ivy, who waved a hand as if to say, *What will be will be.*

When he persisted, she quipped dramatically, "How in *Heaven's* name would I know, Gordon? I deal in e-mail and RSS feeds." In true Web fashion, Ivy claimed she had never taken notice of the pickup time.

Gordon made a quick decision to remain truant from his cubicle and risk a reprimand so that he could hang about on Floor Fifty-Eight, keeping tabs on the outbox there. Simpler than having to make lengthy explanations to Chandler, Gordon told himself. For all her coffee breaks and gossip, she was the department head. But even on Floor Fifty-Eight, he realized, he could spend only so many hours of the day before some supervisor in expensive jeans and Pumas came by and asked what he was working on, mistaking Gord for one of his own, perhaps assuming that his suit was a thrift-store statement.

When, sure enough, this very thing occurred, Gord rolled up his shirtsleeves and ran his hand through his hair, spiking it up at the back. "Conceptualizing, conceptualizing . . . ," he said, gesturing, tempted to add *dude* or *man* to the end of the sentence but unsure it would play. He left this hanging and tried on his Totally Deep look, the one he had perfected a lifetime ago, in junior year, when he had weighed one-twenty and worn black jeans.

Pumas was pleased, or pleased enough, nodded a shagged head that was only slightly more primped than Gordon's, and went away. Gordon was a watch-pot again. When Pumas came back in another hour, Gordon said he had sought a consultation session with someone from Editorial.

"I'm just waiting for Gordon Small to come up."

Pumas punched him on the shoulder and kept on going.

The outbox pickup came at 2:16 that afternoon.

It was a cart and a boy like a small burrowing animal — James Ames, according to his name tag. His eyes were cokey, his skin pale. He looked on the verge of a nosebleed, and his smile appeared drawn on. Gordon scrutinized the lack of care the boy took when he dumped the Floor Fifty-Eight outbox on top of his freight. The corner of one of Gordon's envelopes jutted over the edge of the cart like the silver-pink fin of a salmon jumping out of the stream toward the inevitable. Gordon found himself grinning at Ames — a Bentley-esque exposing of teeth, barely amicable.

"Just heading out myself." Gordon called the elevator, climbed in first, and depressed the Open Door button until the cart was wedged in with him.

He watched as Ames took out an ultimate swipe, the plastic bar on a long coil of wire locked around his workman-brown belt loops. Gordon trailed him through ten other pickups, the wheeled barrel becoming even more perilously stuffed. Ames never questioned Gordon's presence as Gordon patiently held the elevator during each floor's trip.

"I'll bet you get amazing benefits working in mail . . ."

"'Snot bad." Ames shrugged. "Came to work one day with my dad. Musta been short 'cause they hired me on the spot. I been workin' mail since I was sixteen."

Gordon thought he looked it.

"Had to clear eighteen to get benefits, but I been here four years now, and I'll pro'lly never leave."

Gordon supposed that was likely quite true. "Worth dropping out of school for?" he asked, for his own amusement.

Ames started going through the mail on the straight drop down, sorting the envelopes by sizes. "Don't really need tenth-grade math for this." A couple of envelopes fell over the side, Gordon's one of them. Gordon picked them up, hiding his annoyance as he bent, then straightened and handed them back to Ames.

"Goodbye, integers," he quipped.

Ames stared at Gordon, dazed. "Goodbye? You getting off here?" He glanced up at the row of numbers, which continued to click down with no sign of pause.

"No, I'm just saying I agree. One hundred percent."

"Oh. Okay. Sure."

The elevator hit bottom. The doors seeped into the sides and Ames hefted the big plastic cart through them backwards. Quickly turning, he pulled it along behind him by one straggly arm. It dropped a bread-crumb trail of letters as he went. Gordon grabbed them and followed. If Ames heard Gordon's footsteps over the rumbling of the hauled load across concrete, he didn't let on. The tub roared toward a set of coral doors. Ames swung them open, plowing the plastic drum of postage through.

Between the rubber seals of the door, a white, spherical, and symmetrical milieu came into view. Human handlers were sorting and dumping letters into bowling-alley ball-return-style machines that routed the paper materials down twister slides. There was a faint *clack-clack*, like a single metronome in motion. Like Ames, all of the workers were covered from head to toe in UPS brown.

Ames wheelbarrow-dumped his load onto a sorting table and a woman with hands like windmills began riffling through it. Soon the packages were arranged by postal code. One stack went onto this conveyor, one stack onto that one, and the salmon fin of Gordon's writing swam along. He watched it zoom through the bowling-alley technology. At the end of the line a fuchsia square of eye glimmered, read it, logged it instantly, and the envelope dropped out of Gordon's sight through a slot only two fingers wide.

"Where does it go?" Gordon asked Ames, grabbing his arm and gesturing to the slit at the far end of the room. Ames had been about to leave, the mail cart in mid-rotation.

"Where do you think?"

Gordon stood blinking.

Ames rapped the cart. "'Nother cart like this one. But lined with a bag. They come, they pick up the sack, they leave the cart, off it goes. Each of the bags has the country and region. You got your international, national north, west, northwest, east, northeast, south, and, of course, central. 'Cept that one." Ames pointed to a slot that looked identical to the others. "That's interoffice. I take those back upstairs myself."

"But how do *they* — whoever they are — get them? Where do they pick them up?"

Ames gave Gordon an impatient look. "'S like Dumpsters on the outside of a building. *They* pull up in a truck, unlock the Dumpster, collect the bags, off it goes. Okay, Mr. Sixty Minutes?"

"You ever seen the pickup?" Gordon asked, adopting Ames's vernacular without meaning to.

Ames scoffed. "What do I care? I'd rather go smoke. Smoke?" Ames offered, retrieving a cigarette package and extending it in Gordon's direction.

Gordon's bottom lip flattened. He shook his head. As often as he now ducked out with Daves, he wasn't convinced about his addiction to holding something burning in the air.

"DO YOU EVER THINK ABOUT where things come from?" Gordon asked Daves. Gordon bent his mouth around the cigarette as if he could capture more of its smoke that way.

"What things?" Daves made a slight dodging gesture, as if Gordon had just thrown a physical object at him from his periphery.

"Manufactured things. Products."

"All the time, my friend. Be hard not to, actually."

Gordon looked at him with surprise as he realized that Daves' cynicism always came out warm as Christmas.

"China. It's all made in China. Even the things that don't say 'Made in,' they're made *of*," Daves emphasized. "I love that, actually, things that say 'Assembled in' 'Distributed by' — even your damn toothpaste tube. Like, what the hell? The things we consume, the parts and ingredients, come from half a dozen places and meet up in Wherever, U.S.A., and someone there slaps them together for six dollars an hour. Freeeak-ing crazy."

"I picked your favourite subject."

"And don't get me started on NAFTA," Daves continued as if Gordon hadn't said a word, "or we'll be here half the afternoon and written up by Chandler, no doubt."

"I've been thinking . . ."

"Let's forget about Mexico for the time being. If the gluten for pet food can come from the other side of the world — no inspection standards — and that winds up getting mixed and bagged in Kansas and shipped to God knows —"

"Like it's arrived from another dimension. For all we know."

Daves paused, as if he'd finally heard Gordon. He bleated the *Twilight Zone* theme. "This is what I'm always trying to tell you." Daves slapped his palm with the back of his other hand, the smoke clenched in the midst of his wide grin. "How can your work have meaning if nobody knows what your work is? It's the tree-falling-in-suburbia thing. If no one hears, how do you know it's made a sound? You used to be able to say you were a carpenter or a salesman or . . . That meant something. Everyone knew what that meant. You say you work in publishing, media — people have no idea. Do you write things? Do you make web pages?"

"No —" Gordon attempted to interrupt. "We're getting off track."

"Do you make digital animations? Do you physically glue the books together?"

"No one else but us knows" — Gordon began to pace the courtyard — "that this building exists." The only way to keep Daves from interrupting him seemed to be to keep moving. "No one knows that there are seventy floors, that HR, IT, Foreign Rights, and Publicity and Promotion are at the top and Printing, Distribution, and Sales at the bottom. No one knows that Proofreading and Design share a floor. No one knows we're located at 12205 Millcreek Industry Park. No one even knows where Millcreek Industry Park is. You Google-Map it and see what you get. No one knows about this friggin' courtyard." With each step, Gordon's voice rose.

"Hey, no worries." Daves put out a concerned hand as Gordon passed him. "Other book companies do."

"Yes, yes." Gordon continued his rounds. "But they've never been here, have they?"

Daves admitted that no, he'd never heard of any of their competitors visiting. "But . . . the readers know." He said this brightly, and to Gordon's ear it sounded with the same assurance with which believers speak of God.

12

"'AND WHEN SHE DID SHE, her face burned.' Shall I continue?"

"Please," Gordon murmured.

Chandler grimaced, forcing one lip corner down so Gordon could see an out-of-line tooth in the bottom row of her otherwise perfect mouth. It floated like a white life preserver against a bank of gum. "You're missing obvious things. Here's page 26, same book: 'He would make love to her as she had never been made love to her before' . . . It's like you've got a love triangle in your brain, these typos always with the extra *she* or *her*."

"Oh, yes," he admitted, but Chandler merely swivelled that red silk bottom in her rose leather chair and continued to the next sticky-noted page. There was as little privacy in Chandler's office as there was in Gordon's work area, or likely *less*, what with one reader or another coming in every hour to pluck a new script from the tower that had been only slightly rebuilt since Chandler's appointment at Heaven. Still, whenever Gordon was there, he felt an impetuous clashing of desires, which he attributed to their first encounter, and to his ongoing experiment to see if he could experience genuine hunger, desire.

As Chandler lectured him on conditional tenses — "*was* versus *were*" — her office held the ever-tremulous glow of a glass cage. It was 70 percent glass: floor-to-ceiling windows stretched behind her, and wire threaded the panel beside the door. The ceiling was a white plastic checkerboard panel, all light fixtures beyond it.

Our gangerous hearts. Our phosphorescent surrounds. A belief in incarnation and paper clips, a simple perfect joining. Gordon held a finger aloft, dug in his pocket for his miniature spiral pad, and took the thought down to use in his writing later. Chandler assumed he was noting his carelessness. She smiled slightly and waited until he had finished writing before tearing into another mistake with an editor's gusto.

"Page 65, '*Marty* must have thought . . .' The heroine's best friend is named *Marla*. You make it sound like she's gallivanting with multiple men. Not to mention that you've confused the words *release* and *realize* throughout the novel. I actually got a letter about that one, Gord." Gordon could tell Chandler was trying hard to be serious when she whipped the actual letter out of the desk and mashed it into the surface in front of him.

"It's ridiculous," she continued. "You can't turn on little old ladies in Minnesota when you edit the wrong word into the love scenes."

"Did I really?" he queried innocently.

"Yes!" she scolded, leaving the piece of correspondence on the desk and flipping intently through the flamingo pink volume in her hands. "Page 101, 'The most violent of male pleasures was blasting through Vincenzo. It was obvious Antonia felt the same way as she pitched against him in a fever, whimpering, her body saying *more, more, more*. Vincenzo braced himself for one final thrust that would bring them both to climax and send them over the edge. "*I love you*," Vincenzo groaned, as he came to *realise* inside her.' 'Came to *realise* inside her'"? Chandler slapped her palm sternly on the desktop. "Come on, Gordon. With your mistake the hero seems like he has a mental disability and has only just clued in to the fact that he's engaging in intercourse!"

Gordon swam in the words (*pleasures, fever, thrust, climax, intercourse*). He squirmed. "Is it *realise* with an *S* rather than a *Z*?" he managed.

Chandler nodded.

"I thought it was a British thing," he said, lamely.

Gordon's explanation fell on ears as porcelain as prayer hands. The lustrous Chandler went hurriedly on, barking out his errors. "Page 117, missing period. Page 138, 'their hands en*twinned*.' Page 146, 'poured her a glass of wind' — *wine*, I think it is. Page 170, 'plunged the top of his tongue into her dewy core and heard her cry of *leasure*.' 'Leisure,' Gordon? Did you maybe mean *pleasure*?"

"Oh yes, most certainly. Pleasure."

"And 'top of his tongue'?" She stuck hers out at him. Pointed, it came to an eloquent pink V, so vulnerable above her chin. She gestured to it with one finger, and Gordon let his eyes feast upon it. He wondered how long she would let him look at her tongue, and he bit his own. Hers disappeared. "*Tip*, Gordon, *tip* of his tongue."

Gordon raised his eyebrows.

Chandler's shoulders fell, and for a moment she looked almost submissive. "I really hate reprimanding my friends," she whispered, gazing across the desk at him with sad doe eyes. "Please don't do this. Don't make me do it again."

She sighed and picked up the novel again. "Here, let's finish quickly so it's over and we can pretend this never happened," she murmured, gentler, a tad defeated. "Page 172, 'A sensation like a giant fish striking his chest' — that should be *fist*. Page 188, 'in the bitch of excitement' — that should be *pitch*. And for your big finale, on page 196, *clitoris* is quite usually spelled with a *T*, not a *D*. If I didn't know you, I'd suspect you dropped these in on purpose. But there, we're done. Come back when you're my friend again, and in the meantime, do your job, *please*." She edged the book and the letter from the irate reader across the desk for Gordon to take to remind him of his misbehaviour. He picked them up along with his official write-up, which was the same shape as a parking ticket. He had been written up by Chandler Goods, and good was exactly what he felt.

Gordon shifted around inside his clothes before he stood. As he shuffled back to his cubicle, he fetched the letter from between his proofing ticket and his badly done novel. Holding the letter up, still in its envelope, he examined the return address, written in a blossoming blue hand: *Mrs. Abigail Mabey*, from the Twin Cities. Postmark, *December 1*. And stamp. A cardinal sitting on a pine bough.

PART III

DECEMBER

THE CAMERA TRAINED on the courtyard showed employee #1299 accepting a cigarette from his co-worker. Lillian could feel two deep lines forming on her forehead. She tapped the golf pencil against her teeth twice. She strode to her desk, where she found the corresponding file. *Small, G.* Flicking past his laughable resumé, she came to some jottings she had made during their interview. *Non-smoker.* She turned and surveyed the monitor again. It was definitely him — she could tell by his quickly creasing suit. Onscreen, he cupped one elbow with his hand and the smoke seemed to rise from their union.

An odd sensation crept up behind Lillian's ear and she placed a hand there firmly, as if trying to catch an insect. When the feeling didn't go away, she used the pencil to scratch the back of her neck.

"What makes a man take up smoking in Heaven?"

She looked around as if expecting an answer. The pencil had left thin red streaks up and down the white skin on the back of her neck. She let the pencil fall to the desk. There were further notes. *Training without incident, one write-up for proofing errors making it to print. Tendency to linger beyond work hours.* She had not yet made a notation that this "tendency" had recently escalated to staying at work overnight. There was no check box for that. Although she had not gone through them minute by minute, the surveillance records showed not much more than reading, all-hours reading, and occasionally writing, but nothing that fell outside of ordinary office behaviour . . .

"What makes a man take up smoking in Heaven?" she asked herself, and the room, a second time.

13

DAVES' HEAD BOBBED over Gordon's partition. His gaze fixed on the written reprimand from Chandler, which Gordon had thumbtacked into the cloth surface of the cubicle wall.

"You gotta watch that, my friend," Daves warned. "Goes in your permanent file." He gestured to the ceiling. "HR," he whispered.

"Oh?" Gordon set down his pen.

"You know, Lillian Payne had a hyphenated name before she got divorced." Daves continued to whisper. "Payne-in-the-ass. But seriously . . . word is she got her job by screwing over the guy who had the position before her. No one knows what happened to him. Disappeared." Daves reached out and loosened the write-up, the tack falling as he did. "Hide that in your desk drawer. There's good heat and there's bad heat. That's the latter. People have been terminated for less."

"No worries," Gordon said, borrowing one of Daves' favourite sayings.

Daves gave him a surprisingly serious look, rolled Gordon's desk drawer open himself, and dropped the warning inside. He made a gesture toward his mouth with two fingers slightly parted. Gordon nodded, and the two of them ambled past row on row of garlanded compartments, bristling green doorways crowned with lumps of mistletoe and fists of plastic holly berries.

"Thirty percent," Daves muttered over his shoulder.

"Thirty percent?"

"Jewish."

"Pardon?" They reached the elevator, where Bentley gave them a pointed glare.

"Our workforce," Daves explained, swiping the two of them into their downward journey. "I've been asking around and I've calculated it. I talked to Design and Internet, and while certainly you've got all the printers and sales nerds, if you estimate the entire building based on our three departments, which are, you must admit, drastically different and therefore broad enough to be an acceptable sample, almost a full third of the company is Jewish, and yet —" He held up his arms to demonstrate his point. The Muzak that accompanied them down was "Silent Night." Wordlessly, "'round yon virgin mother and child" dripped across the mirrored cell, which was strung with gold tinsel, one lost white angel suspended in the centre from a T-bar.

"You didn't ask me."

Daves raised two hands palms up. "You Jewish?"

Gordon shook his head. "You?"

"Half, my dad. Mom's Catholic. Very." He rolled his eyes.

"Still, it's a matter of principle. This ritualized notion of cele-bration. It's been thrust upon us supposedly to keep good cheer and build community within the company. Down on Floor Four they have a whole gingerbread city made of card-board. You know why?"

Gordon shrugged and watched the numbers click down.

"Competition. Floors Four through Eight have a contest. The sales floors always have to compete. It's part of their workmosphere. They each chip in and then they divide into teams and vie, with decorations, for the pot. It's not low stakes either. They probably drum up enough that the winners could vacation together. But guess what."

They hit bottom and stepped out. "What?"

"You know anyone who's taken a vacation yet this year? I mean, it is the freaking holidays right now. Isn't this when you'd think people would want to vacation? But we have quo-tas to make. Essentially, that's what they are. Quotas. And right now they're giving out overtime. So who doesn't want to make overtime? So that means nobody's taking vacation days. Do you know that Americans take less vacation time than any other western country? That's a fact. Why? We feel like we can't. We don't have time. It's built in to our workplace psy-chology. You know it. But hey, no worries. Who needs a day off? Not only that —"

Daves stopped talking long enough to light the same ciga-rette he'd lit the last time they came out into the sky-patch parkette. When Daves opened the package, Gordon had noticed, there were always three — just like in his own bug box of Vivatex, there were always seven, an unending prescription.

Daves put the smoke to his lips, then lit another one off it and passed it to Gordon.

"— but these fools down in sales are spending all their extra time, I mean breaks, lunches, coming in early mornings, staying late — they don't do this during work hours — to decorate the freaking cages they sit in so the company can turn around and post a mini-feature about their enthusiasm on the corporate section of the web site. They'll get their pictures taken. Big whoop. What kind of reward is that?"

Gordon longed to hear profanity in Heaven — a good *fuck*, a drawn-out *shit*, even the odd *bitch* or *bastard*. But lately every time he opened his mouth to say one such word some other word replaced it, rolling off his tongue before he had realized it.

Daves motored on. "They're not making any extra money. It's not money from the company. It's from their own pockets, and they willingly sign themselves over to it. For what? A pat on the back from the Man. Suckers! If it was the lottery part they were interested in, they could just pass the hat every Friday and have an instant sweepstake, without the expenditure of all that energy, don'cha think?"

"But . . . maybe they're just amusing themselves. Maybe they don't give a Shinola about the Man — they're just looking for something more rewarding to do. How interesting is what we do here, Daves, and what do people really do at home anyway?"

"Huh." Daves tilted his head back. He bounced from mountain boot to mountain boot. "Huh," he said again. "The value of the end product, not being alienated from it. I guess if you decide of your own volition to build a manger, the manger has a different value than *Naked Incorporated*. Yeah, okay. Yeah, I'll buy that. But, holly throughout the whole corporation, the Christmas carols — you gotta admit, it's still a bit dictatorial."

Gordon admitted it was. "Especially if you're an atheist."

"Oh, I am," Daves was quick to add. "I mean, I'm *ex*-Catholic. I was never confirmed. They're not getting me. Once it's over, it's over. That's what I've been saying since I was fourteen."

"Mmm." Gordon stooped and sifted through a handful of snow. He felt a sensation. It burned his naked hands, but it didn't hurt or turn them red the way it had when he was alive. "I don't know."

"You got some theory?" Daves nodded, smiling.

"No," Gordon replied. He dropped the cigarette, which sizzled a thin, deep hole into the snowbank at his knee. "I'm not committing one way or the other."

"Oh, that's good. That's rich, covering all the bases." Daves laughed.

Daves was about to head inside again when Gordon stopped him with a question that was simple and direct. This was always the best way to approach Daves. "Do you really want to see what can be done to rock the system?"

For once Daves didn't say anything. He gave Gordon a quizzical look.

"Who reads the books after you typeset them?"

"You're the last eyes, Gordo."

"No one in Production or Design?"

Daves shook his head, a slow grin blooming across his jaw.

"So technically, with the exception of the first and last pages, which might get looked at in sales, we could write anything between the covers and still have these books wind up in stores. . . . As long as we stick to an accurate word count," Gordon pressed on, "so that the books come out to their standard length, 192 pages, no one will know except the readers? And even the readers won't until the book has come home in a shopping bag or arrived via the mail book club. Am I right?"

Daves took out another cigarette, a dangerous act, since it was the very last in his pack. He lit it, cupping one hand around the tobacco and the other around the flame. "It's risky," he said finally, nodding, "but definitely, definitely possible. The sales team is supposed to read them, but they are . . ." He walked around the courtyard and came back, looked Gordon in the eye, and smiled around his cigarette ". . . very distracted this week."

Gordon began to hum "It Came upon a Midnight Clear," and Daves held up his last cigarette like a conductor's wand.

14

GORDON WAS IN DEEP SPACE.

Smile-shaped constellations, the florid orange pudenda of Venus, the flecked irises of spiral galaxies, the light echo of a star shedding its glow on a tower of dust: within the fourteen-inch confines of his screen, the universe was full of allure — and ghosts. The screensaver photographs of whirlpool galaxies and globular clusters rose upon his monitor, majestic and still, then faded into moon, boomerang nebula, and finally Gordon's old friend Earth. It was just a screensaver, but as he watched, Gordon felt the ecliptic passage between awe and apprehension.

He could remember riding in his mother's red Polara, her hair a platinum fountain above the headrest. From the back seat he would stare up endlessly into the blue sky, knowing that beyond it was black, and beyond that, what she assured him every Sunday existed, the pearly gates of eternity. And here Gordon was on Earth-not-Earth, and he had arrived here with an application.

Outside the windows of the Heaven Book Company, if Gordon stood and gazed at the sunset, he could see that same maculate moon rising, huge and ordinary. On his screen, when he stopped scrolling, there was Rhea, a moon of Saturn, cratered, dating back 4.5 billion years; Titan, Saturn's largest lunar body; and Tethys, its ancient surface of ice unchanged since the birth of the solar system. Gordon could watch the actual sun set through Georgianne Bitz's horizontal blinds or he could adjust his rolling chair and sit before a Saturnian sunset, the sun below the ring plane and the whole planet little more than a red construction-paper cutout of what a planet ought to be. The Milky Way was something molten, turquoise, a scar of smoke in an LCD sky.

Meanwhile, Daves' screen was filling up with never-ending pipes, labyrinthian, cobalt blue. In Erika Workman's station, a psychedelic corona of light twisted and jellyfished. Jill Fast had a magnifying ball that bounced around her screen identifying random text: *"Oh no!" she gasped. "Oh yes!" he assured her . . . familiar sense of anxiety and despair . . . struggling with a thickness in his chest . . .* In Georgianne's cubicle, palm trees swayed over dinted sands and two white chairs faced ever eastward, then disappeared into a lone desert isle, forlorn rock face clouded with green. On Manos's monitor, an other-side-of-the-screen hand was pressing a never-realized message upon the screen.

Measure what is measurable, and make measurable what is not so, Gordon found himself thinking.

What do the others know about Heaven? Gordon wondered. He pushed back from his desk and wound his way through the cubicles, scanning the tops of his co-workers' heads as if he had X-ray vision. When he arrived in the foyer, he slapped his palm down forcefully upon the tall crescent desk.

"You must know just about everything about everybody," Gordon told Bentley. "Working Reception, I mean."

"It's much more than Reception," Bentley responded warily. "It's assistant to the head of Editorial."

"Oh?" Gordon lingered at the podium.

"As you well know, I help coordinate payroll. I help traffic manuscripts between Copy Editing and Proofreading. I also input all of the worksheets for Chandler — not that she'd care to give me credit for that, but you did notice that you were being paid quite regularly long before she decided to make an appearance. I like to think . . ." Bentley made that clacking sound in the back of his throat: *ta-ta-ta*. "Let me just say . . ." *Ta-ta-ta*. "Well." He settled upon this single word as if it were a sentence articulating his point. "I tend to consider myself the caretaker of this department."

The payroll part at least was true. After achieving full-time status and direct deposit, Gordon had been able to forgo the sorry-ass trek to Job City in the basement. Now his pay stub was prepared by Bentley, either handed to him as he exited the elevator or slotted neatly onto the top of his inbox. Convenience in Heaven, as on Earth, was a privilege.

"So . . ." Gordon rubbed two fingers across his mouth as if something had just occurred to him. "What you're saying is, you've had access to employee records for the entire department for some time — at least until Chandler arrived, that is. That's something." Gordon gave a slight head shake.

"JON."

"Gordon."

"Let me ask you something."

Manos glanced at his watch. "Ok–ay . . ."

Gordon gave him no room to change his mind. He pulled up a rolling chair inside Manos's cubicle.

"Is there a problem, Mr. Small?"

Jon Manos called everyone Ms. and Mr. — Mr. David, Ms. Workman, Ms. Bitz — occasionally shuffling up the first names and the surnames: Ms. Erika, Ms. Jill. So how could Gordon take offence at *Mr. Small?* Part of him did, nonetheless. Was it the way Manos looked at him when he said the surname? Some flicker at the corners of his lips?

"Let me ask you something, *Mr. Manos*," Gordon parroted. He leaned in and Manos leaned away ever so slightly. "When was the last time you —"

"Is this a personal question? Because I draw the line at —"

"The last time you —" Gordon's mouth made a straight line across his face and he let his eyes bulge ever so slightly.

He had Manos's attention now. "The last time I *what?*"

Gordon let the word fall. "Defecated."

"When was the last time I defecated?"

Gordon nodded.

"Yes, I just wanted to make sure that what I thought you said is what you said. . . . I'm not answering that." Manos stood up and made to leave his own workspace.

"Wait, Jon. I'm serious."

Manos paused but didn't sit down again.

"Since I've been in Heaven, my caffeine intake has gone up

ninefold, and — nothing. I don't think I've expelled in the two and a half months I've been here. How can I be swimming in all this coffee and not output any of it? I'm not the only one, either. It's like we're all on speed out there — how do you think we read so fast? We're a reading factory on Fast Forward. But have you ever once heard a sound — a *peep* — in the men's room?"

Manos was listening now, shocked, but listening.

"I dare you. Go into that men's room and just stand at the sink and wait."

Manos stared at Gordon, a horrified expression fastened to his mouth.

"It's nothing but a powder blue holding pen. Men in the stalls. Nothing's happening." Gordon gestured with one hand, flipping it over to show the two sides, palm up and palm down. "We come out, wash our hands, use that liquid lemon soap as if to prove to ourselves that something occurred worth cleaning up, but when was the last time you remember actually sitting down, contorting with the effort of —"

"Enough," Manos rasped as he pushed past Gordon and out of his own cubicle.

GORDON WATCHED AS FLEUR packed her purse with an empty Tupperware lunch container and two new Heaven titles from the freebie shelf. He pretended to be engrossed in the freebie shelf as well. She didn't bother to snap the purse shut, simply hooked its black straps over her shoulder, the salad-oiled plastic nuzzling the crook of her armpit. She folded a lightweight orange leather jacket over her other arm as if she didn't intend to wear it. "Nice clothes, bad skin," was what Gordon had heard the other women in the office say about Fleur when she was out of earshot.

"See you tomorrow," she said over the cubicle wall to Jill.

Gordon armed himself for the elevator ride with three randomly plucked titles. He let Fleur pad toward the elevator in her open-toed pumps, which, he realized for the first time, were incredibly out of season. When she had a fifteen-second lead on him, he followed, scuttling in just before the elevator doors closed.

"I would've held it for you," she said as if she had been accused of something.

"It's okay." He smiled and looked down at his hands. Two of the books he held were from the Secret Hearts imprint; the other was from Second Love, a line that featured mid-life romances and the carousing of divorcees. When he glanced up, he saw that Fleur had followed his eyes. "Mom," he explained with a shrug that he hoped conveyed just a touch of embarrassment. "She likes the mysteries."

"I worked on that one," Fleur said, examining the spine. "It's cute."

"Cute's good."

Fleur smiled weakly. "Weekend plans?"

Gordon shook his head. "You?"

"The girls. Bar. A new one I read about." She continued to smile idly as others got on and rode down. When Gordon and Fleur exited into the parking garage, it was natural for them to walk together. She clicked across the concrete beside him. "You don't usually drive, do you?"

"No," he replied. "Just today."

The disruption to routine didn't seem to faze her.

The parking garage had an alphabetical organization to it: concrete pillars hung with large placards: A, B, C. Spots were assigned to employees alphabetically. Fleur's surname began with J, so it was natural that she would come to her spot before Gordon arrived at his. They walked silently, and Gordon felt a strange sense of déjà vu as the bone-coloured lines of the spaces flashed past. For a second, even though Fleur was within arm's reach, he felt alone. The stale air of the parking garage seemed as if it belonged to another garage in some distant time and place. By the time Fleur had rummaged past her salad container and pulled out a ring of noisy keys, Gordon recalled that it was a garage on Bay Street he was remembering, but not why he had been there.

"Thanks for walking me," she said. "I do sometimes find it creepy down here."

"No . . ." Gordon paused. "No problem." His look was inquiring, but she was busy unlocking a hatchback. "Creepy how?" Glancing about them, Gordon noticed for the first time that the lights contained sodium vapour bulbs, that both he and Fleur looked greyish beneath them. His suit, which he knew to be olive, had turned to charcoal. Her orange jacket, smoke.

She got in her car, closed the door, strapped herself in, and waved as Gordon headed off casually in the direction of S.

He had walked only as far as K before he concealed himself on the other side of a pillar. The hatchback still hadn't started its engine. None of the cars in the garage had started their engines, even though people were entering their vehicles all around him. Gordon wondered if each driver was waiting for the one next to him to exit. When he ducked around the pillar to look back at Fleur's spot, she was still sitting in the driver's seat in the same position he'd left her, a slightly strained smirk on her face, staring straight ahead.

An hour later, all of the other cars were full — and none had moved.

Gordon headed back to Fleur's vehicle. He stood in front of it, staring through the windshield. She stared back at him but gave no indication of seeing him. He walked over to her side, crouched beside her window, and peered in. Her head didn't turn. He tapped the glass. He pressed his face against it until his nose and cheek mashed. He turned backwards, bent, and knocked his bum against the window three times in succession with a slight hip-shake. He tried the handle, but she had locked it after herself. He withdrew. He turned in a circle, taking in the sheer number of cars, of heads against headrests, of eyes.

GORDON FOLLOWED THE CUBICLES in order. When collecting data, one should be systematic, he told himself. He did not think of his method as hunting and gathering so much as provoking and proving. Observing reactions. For Fleur, there was a stack of mauve sticky notes, each scrawled with an identical message. Every morning he thumb-rubbed one onto the face of her computer: *How did you sleep?* For Carma, there was a stack of e-mail messages in Gordon's drafts box preprogrammed to be sent each afternoon at 5:27, three minutes before day-end.

For Erika, there was a music playlist Gordon had downloaded and recorded up in the Internet Division: nineteen tracks of death. For Rachel, there was a memo advising her to make careful note of the number of times per day she urinated (Gordon already knew the answer: zero). For Jill, there was a bowl of rat poison Gordon had located in the basement — though he doubted there were any actual rats in Heaven. It looked so pretty next to the sugar canister in the kitchen. For Fiona, a birthday card with a skull and crossbones pencilled beneath a trite humourous Shoebox message.

It ought to have been easy for Gordon to convince himself of his shadow existence, especially when he had all the evidence. He did not eat, drink, or sleep any more. He did not bleed. He did not excrete in a normal manner. He did not sweat or salivate. He did not breathe. He did not process pain. His bones and muscles were malleable place holders. He still perceived smells and tastes, and had enough circulation to produce a firm reaction of arousal, but he believed these sensations to be little more than memories retrieved from some part of his brain that still longed for life. Echoes. It seemed that whatever was left of Gordon was up to him.

HE COULD SEE BENTLEY loosening. Every day Bentley was waiting for him. And every day Gordon delivered his standard hello. Their greeting had grown from an obligation into an insult, then had progressed into a strange territory between friendship and conniving, falling so distinctly in the middle that even Gordon wasn't sure if he meant it genuinely. *Everyone wants something,* Gordon told himself. *If you want to know what, look for whatever it is they don't have.* Thinking back over the games Bentley had played with him, Gordon deducted, power. But also, friends. Strange, he thought, how Bentley's desire for one seemed to cancel out the possibility of the other.

"Morning," Gordon trilled as he approached the podium. He stopped and leaned upon it, inquiring about the type of vehicle Bentley drove, coveting it aloud, though the vehicle Bentley referenced was as ordinary as the next. Gordon shook his head, repeated Bentley's brand again, as though it were smoother than sliced bread.

He determined to shake in a few derogatory comments over the next couple of days about Chandler's work habits and perhaps her entire gender, and in less than a week's time, Bentley would be his fastest friend.

GORDON WATCHED CHANDLER through the webbed glass: her hand upon the computer mouse, the last three fingers raised slightly, pinky out as if taking tea. Her face was awash with the screen's glow and her eyes had a questing look to them. All whites. The skin about her eyes was stunningly supple, without wrinkles. Her mouth was a tender pink ring, without lipstick, smooth, just gloss. Gordon watched the mouth change as he swung into her office, his fingers still hooked around the door frame, a simple lean-in. Poised for greeting, the words that came out of his mouth to change the shape of hers were *"Bon matin, nous sommes morts."*

She wrinkled her brow at him.

The next day, the same scene, but in English: "Good morning, we're dead."

Chandler's lips gripped themselves up into the corners. She paused, then gave Gordon a tentative wave.

And the next day, again in French: *"Vous êtes morte."*

A head nod.

English: "You are dead."

A finger gun sent him on his way.

French: *"Oui, vous êtes encore morte."*

A blank stare.

English: "Yup, still dead."

Her eyes remained fixed on the screen.

Encore en français: "Bonjour, la mort."

She stood up, crossed the space in two strides, and closed the door, nearly on his fingers.

On the seventh day, Gordon rested.

"IT'S NOT ENOUGH." Daves offered up the printed files of their secret project. Blocking the entrance to Gordon's cubicle, he flipped through the layouts and spoke quietly but without paranoia. "I mean, it can be, if you don't want to knock out as much of *Darling Deception*, leave a bit more than the first and last page, plunk your text somewhere in the middle, say. But, uh, I think that's more likely to confuse the reader. Wha'd'you think?"

"I can write some more," Gordon assured him. "How much?"

Daves shrugged, slapped a palm against his jeans, eyeballs slanted toward the ceiling, accessing the part of his brain that was good with physical space, estimation. "You've already got a hundred pages, so . . . another hundred?"

Gordon nodded. *Not a problem.* "When does it start thinning out around here for the holidays?"

"Well, I'll be in. Buncha the Designs will too. Should get pretty quiet soon though. Say we've got about a week 'til the office is clear. Bear in mind, even once we push this through, it'll take a while to get out. There's some lag time. I mean, Heaven distribution is something, but it's just the nature of shipping, and then receiving and stocking once it gets to the stores. You ever work on that end?"

Gordon shook his head. He'd done enough ordering for Whoopsy's, but he didn't think he could equate it with bookstore experience.

"From what I can tell, book-club readers are gonna get theirs first. I'd say, once it goes out the door . . . probably about a month before management gets wind of it."

Manos's capped head bobbed outside the cubicle opening, and Daves greeted him with a head nod without breaking a sweat. "See the top of this page, how it falls in layout . . ." Daves leaned into Gordon's cubicle, opening their fake manuscript randomly and pointing with his thumb. The way he leaned blocked the pages from Manos's view. "Should there be a paragraph break? You're the proofreader, you tell me." Manos passed without incident.

Gordon arched his eyebrows at Daves' ingenuity but said nothing. He flipped the pages, examining his own words type-set. He had been judicious in his use of profanity to be sure it didn't pop from the page, causing undue suspicion in the casual skimmer.

"You know, that's some freaked-up horse pucky there, Gord," Daves remarked, hooking one elbow over the parti-tion, borrowing some of Gordon's least favourite Heaven Books slang. "Kinda makes me worry about you. It's, uh, it's good writing, and I'm happy to help, don't get me wrong. I just . . ." Daves shook his head. "It's a novel, yeah? Fiction? I mean, it *is* fiction, right?"

"I had a book once . . ." Gordon said as he stared at the page.

"You have a book?" Above Gordon's head Daves was sud-denly all smiles, as if Gordon's flights into fancy could now be forgiven.

"I did."

"That's amazing. So, this is, like, your follow-up?"

The page that lay open before them contained a full run of suicide statistics. Gordon had included them for reasons even he himself didn't comprehend. The line about 20 percent of

U.S. suicides being from toxification (poisoning and over-dose) jumped out at him. As did the causes: depression, pain (physical or emotional, non-correctable), stress (grief, guilt, failure), crime, mental illness, substance abuse, adverse environment, financial loss, sexual issues (including unrequited love and breakups).

"You might say that."

15

TIME WAS LONGER IN HEAVEN. Boredom had driven Gordon to many dull and desperate things in his lifetime: whistling, learning to spit far distances, marijuana, masturbation, masturbation involving fruit, alcohol, prescription drugs, several combinations thereof, overeating, undereating, shoplifting, medieval literature, Roland Barthes, William S. Burroughs, pornography, acoustic guitar, foreign films, and even sports in his youth, though on the field he never held much more command than a blade of grass. In the latter part of high school and shortly after, there were even girls — girls for practice. Practice girls. Nice girls he should have thought himself lucky to get. Girls with big teeth and small breasts. Girls who probably went on to be knockouts when they were more confident and had dated guys less selfish than he. (He'd wondered at first if Chloe might be one of those, and he hadn't always returned her calls, as if to convince himself she was.) But of all these things, by far the most impetuous cure for boredom Gordon had ever attempted was his current self-imposed reading of romance novels. Still, it beat watching the TV in the Floor Six gym, which broadcast business and health reports he wouldn't have paid attention to while alive, and which doubly lost their meaning after death. Options were limited. Gordon had his own mind to entertain him, or the romance novels.

Into his upturned eye Gordon emptied the last of the bottle of Visine he had thought to bring in his first day. Tomorrow, Gordon knew, a miraculous eighth-inch of clear liquid would appear at the bottom of the container again.

For the first half of *Express Male*, the author had adopted the word *rueful* as her top choice, using it at least eight or nine times and, in one instance, twice in the same paragraph. Abruptly, at page 100, the author had turned on her heel (an act that was, Gordon had long ago noticed, so popular in the genre) and began using the world *whilst* with the same — or even greater — lack of discretion. The text paraded like a poem of *whilst* across the screen until his eyes swam:

> Whilst she was turning on her heel, he caught her sash and her robe fell open. Whilst a flame rose in her porcelain cheeks, so her nipples also glowed. He caught her delicate wrist in his hand and reeled her, without protest, to him whilst she blushed.
>
> "Oh," she murmured silkily whilst he freed more of her ivory shoulders, her taut buds erect between his fingers, feeling his touch with every fibre of her being. Whilst he fondled her, her head lolled dizzily on the column of her throat. She moaned whilst he

rubbed. She gasped whilst he suckled. She sang whilst he squeezed.

He apologized enthusiastically whilst bringing their bodies flush.

"Don't be sorry," she confessed reassuringly whilst she stripped his shirt over his head.

"Damn and double damn," he breathed in savage relief whilst she ran her palms over his muscular torso.

Whilst she gazed, he hardened. Whilst he hardened, she gazed. It was as if his whole body had moved up into a higher gear whilst she stroked him lower and lower. A gasp of air escaped her lips whilst he struggled to control his burgeoning passion. She released the thick telltale ridge of flesh from beneath his Parasucos whilst he begged her to think of the consequences. Whilst her busy fingers worked his shaft ever stiffer, he intimately stroked her eager arousal, finding a sensitive place inside her she'd never known existed. He was dangerously aware of her womanscent whilst she bent her head, silky locks falling against his burning flesh. Whilst she licked him, he licked her.

Dance whilst the music still goes on. Get it whilst it's hot. Get it whilst you can. Whilst you loved me. Whilst you were sleeping. Take me for a little whilst, I've got to make you love me, for a little whilst. Whilst the gettin' was good. Whilst you see a chance take it, find romance, fake it. 'Scuse me whilst I kiss the sky.

Whilst my guitar gently weeps. How wonderful life is whilst you're in the world. Whistle whilst you work.

It was close to five when Bentley appeared outside the cubicle, partway between Proofreading and Design. He beckoned to Gordon, a shifty look on his face. He obviously expected Gordon to come near enough for him to whisper — closer to his bent neck than Gordon would have liked. "What kind of man are you?" Bentley finally rasped. "Can you keep quiet?"

Gordon had known it: Bentley's secrets were bigger than he was. Holding up innocuous hands, Gordon made no reply, which he had always found the best defence for later when — as was often said in the books of Heaven — "the fit hit the shan."

Bentley made his insecure tsking — that *ta-ta-ta* sound like fingers drumming on a table — in the back of his throat. He glanced over his hunched shoulder. "Come on," he said. One flaking finger twitched vaguely as he strode between the two departments, detoured past his own station, and finally headed down the hall beside Chandler's office. Gordon held his breath and followed in Bentley's drafty wake.

Bentley swiped them through a doorway requiring an elaborate punch code, which Gordon took care to memorize. Then they found themselves before the only thing Gordon had faced in Heaven that was not white, pink, powder blue, or gold: an immense oak door that had been painted, and repainted, black. Its surface was as thick and cracked as charcoal.

Unlike the rest of Heaven, the file room was accessed not by a code but by an old-fashioned key. Gordon stood very still as Bentley fussed with the lock. As he waited, Gordon silently repeated to himself the punch code he had just watched Bentley finger in. He didn't know what Bentley was about to show him, but he suspected it was something vital to his understanding of how he had arrived and, possibly, if he would ever leave.

The code already felt snug in his mind, more like a colour than a combination; all he had to do to recollect it was to envision its brightness, and its name would follow. Gordon had found that remembering the things that happened here was much easier than remembering the far past, and wondered if this was part of the reason his co-workers were so reluctant to call up their life stories and talk of their neighbourhoods, partners, or children, bantering instead about brands and pop songs, which held a glorious newness. The company's own web site was replete with sponsored iTunes ads and promotions, and the gym's television fed them with information about fresh wars that were so very much like old wars whose details the employees barely recollected. Gordon pursed his lips and recalled the code one more time for safekeeping.

Bentley smiled over his shoulder, his grin no longer seeming hostile to Gordon, but sexual and conspiratorial. The steel handle turned beneath his reedy fingers. "Not a word," he cautioned. "It would mean our jobs."

How much Bentley's job meant to him Gordon wasn't sure. Even if he didn't comprehend his own lack of heartbeat, it was clear that Bentley knew, if not as much as Gordon, a great deal about Heaven.

The black door swung open. The smell of sawdust and autumn leaves greeted them, along with a library silence. The fusty room was little more than a narrow corridor tucked in behind Chandler's office. But unlike those environs filled with tremulous sunlight, the file room ended without so much as a window.

Bentley reached inside and fumbled for a switch. The fluorescents were naked and hung much lower than they did elsewhere in the building. They came on, snapping and sputtering inside their tubes, which were a moonlike blue-white. Gordon saw that the hall carpet stopped just inside the doorway without so much as a piece of trim on the threshold. Beyond the ragged edge, a checkerboard of tiles in rose and white rubbed faded shoulders with one another. On either side of the aisle filing cabinets stood, eight feet tall. At the very end, against a raw concrete wall, sat an old wooden swivel chair, its seat and back marred with streaks of white paint as if someone had attempted to stand upon it while working overhead with a dripping brush. Bentley swept his arm back. *After you*, the gesture said.

Gordon hesitated, then walked down the spine of the skeletal room.

Behind him a tired drawer screeched open. Gordon whipped around and watched as Bentley's fingers flicked absently through velvet dust that floated up from the drawer's fan of pink folders. "They date back to 1965. Every employee we've had here in Editorial, and not just resumés either. Heaven is very comprehensive." Bentley raised an eyebrow — a full-grown brown mouse dashing across his forehead.

"Impressive." Gordon ran his thumb along the line of drawers, leaving a bare black stripe where he passed. He stopped at one marked *Ga–Go*.

"It's not, actually," Bentley continued. "The company was founded in 1955 with the rise of the housewife, the notion of the idle partner behind the picket fence, the boom of post–World War II industry — *i.e.*," he emphasized, "plenty of walk-around-town money. That's ten years that have gone missing, so there's no knowing who worked at the original Heaven building or how things were done for that first, important decade that established the company as one of the top publishing houses in the world."

Gordon had wrenched open the G's and was in the process of crab-walking through the soft edges of folders when Bentley's words sunk in. "The original Heaven?"

"From what I can tell from the very oldest of the files, it used to be located somewhere to the east of the parkway." Bentley shrugged his lopsided shoulders. With the movement he struck Gordon suddenly as sheepish, immense with insecurity, an actual ally.

"Who was head of Editorial before Chandler?" From the drawer Gordon pulled a slick, unwrinkled file labelled *Goods*.

"Diamond-Blume, Melanie. Before her, O'Donnell, Tess. And before that, Schneider, Seth. And . . . let's see . . . a Miss Rebecca Noble." Bentley closed the *B* drawer he had opened, which likely bore his own file, and strode past Gordon, liberating the N's and producing Miss 1965's file almost immediately, in spite of its crumbling edges. Bentley's skull-like face flushed. "It's . . . it's *my* system," he admitted, stammering just a little, his embarrassment coupled with pride. "Believe me, if I had been here in '65 everything would be filed properly, nothing ever would have been incomplete, but . . ." His black eyes burned with regret. "I started in '66. The building was still brand new, yet everything was in chaos. I don't know who was in charge in that intervening year. But some things" — his voice dropped — "some things could not be recovered."

"Since '66, huh? Is it true that a window hasn't been opened here in thirty years?" Gordon jerked open the S drawer and found his own file too easily, the type on it still fresh, the folder edges not yet dogged. He pinched it between thumb and forefinger, tugged it up slightly, then let it fall back. He closed the drawer without removing the folder.

"No." Bentley laced his fingers together and cracked them before taking them for another lightning whirl through the files. "Because they were pinching pennies, they replaced the windows ten floors at a time over a period of seven years. They started in '68, so technically" — he beamed — "it's been thirty-*four* years."

"Do you know about the employees on other floors?"

An eerie smile split Bentley's crooked face so that he resembled the Titus whom Gordon had always known.

"You mean HR?"

Gordon allowed himself to nod.

Bentley shook his head but the smile still hung from his nose. "Unfortunately, all of the departments are separate. Design has a separate room tucked in behind the supervisor's office over there." Bentley gestured vaguely, pointing back through the black door. "Different key. But I can tell you one thing." He shut the drawers they had opened and handed the files to Gordon to browse, which he did. "Lily Payne..."

"Yes?" The word clicked in Gordon's throat, like a token falling into a slot.

With its reception, Bentley's information came out. "... has been here *at least* as long as I have." Bentley pressed his palms together in front of his chest. "You might say she's —" He stopped himself and closed his eyes, nodding as if coming to terms with the idea of passing on the information. "She has aged remarkably well."

GORDON REALIZED HE HAD — consciously or subconsciously, he wasn't sure which — skipped making Georgianne Bitz part of his research. Now he headed toward her cubicle, wondering if the smell of her lunch would meet him halfway there.

Something sat upon Georgianne's desk, but it was not a tuna-fish sandwich. It was a gold-plated frame. It held the image of the face that covered the mind that had dreamed up the very idea of tuna fish.

The child was a kind of Everychild: a child with Chiclets for teeth, with the thin yellow film across them common to those who gorge on orange drink and animal crackers; sandwiched into a coral-and-red-plaid cowgirl shirt, a shirt her mother had obviously selected for her, and which was probably worn over a white cotton camisole with tiny roses embroidered on the neckline; wearing a lopsided grin as if the photographer had at the last minute said something sort of funny but not really, perhaps creepy-funny, though she wasn't sure; whose hair had been pinned behind her ears with shiny brown barrettes positioned as accurately upon her head as if a level had been used, yet whose strands were still static at the very ends, near her pointed collar; whose eyes shone like the flashbulb that lit them; whose ears were in need of a Q-tip; whose cheeks were like felt-covered ping-pong balls; who was obviously studying cursive; who had no idea what she wanted to be when she grew up but was certain she would be an amazing success; who nicknamed the other children and felt shamed when they nicknamed her back; who, Gordon imagined, had written *Left* and *Right* in green marker on her palms and was extremely relieved to discover that her hands would not show in the photo, because she believed herself to be just slightly too old for such prompts.

"How old is your daughter, Georgianne?"

"Eight. Why?"

"And how old was she when you started working here?"

Georgianne gave Gordon a doubtful look. "Eight."

"How long have you been working here, Georgianne?"

Perplexity. "Oh, I don't know! A while."

"Eight years, George. You've worked at Heaven Books for eight years." Gordon held up the work records from Bentley's file room. "In another two years they'll give you a little gold clock for your desk."

"That's not possible." Georgianne put her hard mouth on and spun away from Gordon, ignoring him and the paper evidence.

He picked up her extension. "Call your daughter."

"What are you trying to prove?"

Gordon nodded at the phone, his nice-guy face on. Georgianne relented.

"Jolene, honey, just wanted to call and see how you are . . . Sure, sweetheart, a couple of hours." Georgianne nodded to Gordon across the cord, smiled as if to say, *See? All normal.* "Uh-huh . . . uh-huh . . . uh-huh . . . Okay, I promise." She hung up the phone.

"What did she say?"

"Oh, you know, the usual." Georgianne swept some invisible crumbs off her desktop.

"The usual? What did you talk about yesterday?"

Georgianne shrugged.

"Okay, today then?"

"Asked me when I'd be home."

"And when will you be?"

Georgianne looked at her watch. It was thin, silver, with little faux diamonds all around the face. She'd received it for her fifth anniversary at Heaven. "Well, finish here at five-thirty, we live up in Newmarket, so depending on traffic . . ." She shrugged again, a gesture Gordon couldn't recall her using previously.

"Oh, does it get busy out that way?" Gordon played along. "How long on a good day? Forty-five minutes, an hour?"

"What, planning to come for supper?" Georgianne snapped with unusual acerbity. "I've only been getting in six hundred lines an hour lately, Gordon. Sorry, but since I'm a little behind" — she tilted her chin — "you should probably go now."

THE NEXT DAY, at 3:35 p.m. Gordon swung by Georgianne's cubicle.

"Hey Georgy-girl, call your daughter yet today?"

"No," she said, frostily.

"Don't you think you should? See if she liked her lunch? Find out what happened at school, what she wants for supper?"

Georgianne glared at him. "If I didn't know you, Gordon, I would think there was something a little . . ." She searched for the word, glancing at the cubicle wall that she shared with Manos. Her voice dropped. ". . . *queer* about your interest in my daughter."

They both held their ground.

"Okay, I'll call her," Georgianne said when she saw he had no intention of leaving, "if only to show you that our lives are as regular as anyone else's. Not that it's any of your *fu-dging* business." She dialled. "Hi, Jolene, honey . . . Just wanted to call and see how you are . . . A couple of hours," she said, as if around a razor blade in her throat. She hung up the phone quite suddenly.

"Mmm?"

"She asked when I'd be home . . ." Georgianne stared at the telephone morosely.

"That's funny. Didn't she ask you that yesterday?"

Georgianne nodded. "I guess I'm not there enough." Her voice broke and she covered her eyes. "I'm a bad mom."

"No, you're not."

"Well, you must think so, or you wouldn't have come over here two days in a row to prove it to me." She began to sob, thick hiccups curling behind her hand.

Even in his more sensitive days, the Chloe days, the days of Gord and Chloe, Gordon Small had not been so good with tears. But now he moved with the kind of ease that comes when one knows there aren't consequences to touch. He placed one hand on Georgianne's shoulder — a nubby knit — and held onto it, for as long as needed, as long as it would take for her to stop. She didn't stop.

"You're not a bad mom, Georgianne. It's just that you're..."

She stopped and looked up.

Gordon let go. "...dead."

"Fuck," Georgianne said, uttering the first real curse he had heard since he'd been at Heaven.

16

AN HOUR LATER Gordon found Georgianne Bitz with her hands in the kitchen sink. "What is that?"

"What does it look like?"

"A bra."

"Very good. Gold star."

"You're washing your bra in Sunlight?"

"Well, where are you washing your clothes? I mean, if I haven't been home in eight years, I'm obviously not washing them there, so . . ." Between her furious thumbs the white nylon scrunched with suds. "I — I can't live knowing that. What's your secret?"

Gordon looked down. He couldn't say that he wasn't washing, that he hadn't washed the suit — or his gotchies — in however many months had passed since he'd arrived.

He wondered, actually, not counting trailing after Chandler Goods and harassing every co-worker like a post-apocalyptic prophet preaching in reverse, what *had* he been doing?

THAT EVENING GEORGIANNE came to find him. Gordon looked up, and above his cubicle wall her face, like a bad oil portrait, floated inside the crooked brown frame of her hair, which had come half undone. She had been crying without any tears. The scientist in him wondered what that felt like.

"I don't know what to do." Her voice sounded as though it had been poured through heavy cheesecloth; slowly it filtered through.

Gordon turned away from his computer, whose clock read two minutes until quitting time. "You can do what you've always done, or you can do something else."

"But . . . what did I always do?" Georgianne's forehead scrunched into her eyebrows and the bridge of her nose so that it wasn't simply a stitch that appeared, but an elaborate archway of lines.

"You went down to the parking garage as if you were going home."

"How do you know? Did — did you follow me?" Her voice carried a note of suspicion.

Gordon shook his head. "Fleur."

"But you suspect I'm the same?"

Gordon lifted one shoulder. "She got into her car. She sat at the wheel, staring out past the dashboard. Eventually she fell asleep. I suspect, though" — Gordon paused — "her eyes were open. . . . The same is true of Jill and Jon. I've only been down once in the middle of the night. I find it kind of creepy, to tell you the truth. To turn in a circle and see everyone sitting in their vehicles like that, just staring out. Like they're inside recharging pods." He shook his head to clear the image from his mind. A thought occurred to him, and he leaned toward her, his hands between his knees. "Do you dream there? Do you remember dreaming?"

Georgianne lowered her eyes, which were heavily wrinkled. Today, for reasons Gordon understood, she looked closer to fifty than forty. "I don't know. I think I'm in shock. After what you've told me, I don't remember anything."

"Try going down tonight. See if you do."

He meant it earnestly, but the smile she presented to him was tired and twisted. "What, are we pathologists now?"

"Well, there's TV and radio in the gym, if you prefer that. And the Net Division on Floor Fifty-Eight has every entertainment you could want. But if you're hoping to spend the night there, you'll have to hurry. It's not accessible after 5:40, so you've got less than ten."

"Thank you, Gordon." Georgianne reached out and patted Gordon's head as if he were a child. "Thank you so much for sharing with me. Tell me something else . . ."

He waited her out. Given the tone she had adopted, he wasn't about to make any more suggestions.

"Do you know how I died?"

He said nothing.

"So you do, because you haven't denied it. Let's see: fire, drowning, illness, unexpected tumor — strike that, I'd definitely remember — stroke . . ." Georgianne folded down a finger with every suggestion. "Suicide, murder, death by lightning, act of terrorism, plane crash, car accident — Ah, there it is, that's the one. I can see it all over you. Thanks,

Gordon. Thanks again. You've been a real dear." She walked stiffly away, leaving Gordon with the distinct impression that one of his few confidants in Heaven had no intention of speaking to him for the rest of eternity.

At around ten at night Gordon rose from his computer and left his cubicle. Pocketing and unpocketing his hands, he ventured around the floor. It was his hope that Georgianne might have had enough hours alone to absorb the trauma and would be willing to talk to him again.

How long do you need to shake off the shock of your own mortality? Is it a longer process than that of other traumas? he asked himself as he walked through the kitchen. He opened the fridge — as if there would be some tuna evidence of Georgianne there — pulled out an apple that did not belong to him, inspected it, rubbed it against his shirt, and bit, all the while concluding that he himself might be in shock even now. Nonetheless, he continued his search for Georgianne. A part of him wished it had been Chandler who had clued in. But he knew she wasn't constructed that way. Chandler was hard-wired for denial. It was part of her optimism. He looked for Georgianne in the Design Department, the cafeteria, the gym, even down in the courtyard where he regularly ashed with Daves. Gordon narrowed his eyes at Security as he passed the station, but the guy didn't look up from the *Auto Trader* he had been reading for three months.

Gordon debated ducking into the parking garage to see if Georgianne had followed his advice. He knew she drove a coffee-brown Saturn. The idea of going down there and wandering among the cars gave him the heebie-jeebies; still, he stepped into the elevator and pressed the appropriate button. When the doors parted, he caught a whiff of gasoline and immediately shielded his eyes with one hand, hit Close Doors, and commanded the lift to take him to the other level of the basement, the one that led to the Passage.

Once, when Gordon was alive, he had wound up in the basement of a hospital. He had gone alone to visit his aunt because his mother hadn't been able to make it that day. When he went to exit, he'd asked a nurse for directions to place him outside the building, closest to where he had parked. Her instructions, though direct, had unkindly sent him down to the entranceway to the morgue. He had stepped off the elevator and stopped short, as if exiting into a brick wall. He had known the smell of the dead when it hit, and it sent an instant dread through his nostrils and down his throat. It had been enough to make Gordon want to spin right around again and retreat. Had it been a smell, he wondered now, or simply a vibe? A gut feeling? The doors to the morgue were unmarked, yet Gordon had believed without a doubt that that was where he was. A young orderly with a gurney had rattled by at that moment, and though the stretcher carried equipment, not a human form, beneath that pale green cloth, the orderly had given Gordon a look of empathy embedded in warning, as if he did not wish Gordon to see what lay beyond the double doors he was heading toward. He'd jerked his head in the other direction and said simply, "That way."

Gordon didn't smell the tang of the terminated now; he was one of them. But the trancelike austerity of the parking garage at night, with its concrete and arrows and all its unseeing eyes, sent him into the same state of uncanny quivering. It made his ears well with static. It raised the hairs along his spine and rocked his stomach from side to side. Was it his form of denial, to not be able to join the rest of the dead?

He exited instead into the first basement, located a garbage can, and disposed of the sticky core that was left of the apple. Then, tentatively, he edged along the Passage and pushed open the door of the bra and underwear manufacturer he'd spotted on an earlier trip. Row on row of machines clacked behind a partition. When she spotted him through the plate glass, a woman with a clipboard exited the workroom to stand behind a counter. "What do you need?" she yelled over the racket of needles plunging through polyester.

Gordon wasn't sure. Mentally he was picturing Chloe's breasts — he still knew her size — and comparing them to Georgianne's. But the process of deducing that Georgianne was likely a few inches larger around and a cup size or two up also required Gordon to picture Georgianne's breasts in his hands, to physically weigh them against Chloe's.

"What do you need?" Clipboard barked again.

"Something for a friend." She gave him a look as if that went without saying. "C, I think."

"Thirty-two? Thirty-four? Thirty-six? Forty?" The woman ran through the sizes like a football quarterback; Gordon expected her to add a "hup" to the end. Instead, with exasperation, she produced a number of garments from the bins behind the counter and he pointed dumbly to the ones that looked right. He took three, to be on the safe side. All were white, since he didn't want his gesture misinterpreted. As he swiped his debit card, he pictured the plain brassieres neatly arranged in a row on Georgianne's desk. In his mind a neon sticky note attached itself to one vacant mesh boob. What would he write on the Post-it? *Downstairs, First Basement, Tunnel A.* Or maybe, *An apology.*

Afterward, lavender shopping bag in hand, Gordon headed toward the immense mailroom where Ames worked and communication conveyor-glided.

Like the stitchers in the sewing factory next door, the postal workers laboured all hours. Their energy and noise buoyed Gordon, and every so often he came down to the tunnel just to hear the clack of their machines and the sound of their laughter. Why they seemed more human, less repressed than all of the workers up on Twelve, he could not say. Perhaps it was because they weren't helping to create fantasy twenty-four hours a day; they were simply moving. Their fingers whirled over postal codes. Their minds remained their own. He had learned that if he leaned in, dressed in his suit as he was, the inhabitants of the mailroom were likely to assume one of two things: that he was a lost employee from upstairs or that he was managerial, visiting from somewhere off-site, sent in momentarily to check up on them. In either case, he was pleasantly ignored.

Tonight he had only barely nudged open the doors when a bulbous woman turned around to face him. All abdomen, she stood at the table nearest him, a sheaf of envelopes in her hands. On the bottom she was wearing the same shade that cloaked her co-workers, a below-the-knee chocolate work skirt. Unlike them, she had been permitted to wear a bone-coloured cotton blouse. Wraparound, it tied on one side, the fabric lingering tautly upon the ridge of her inflated belly, riding up just enough that Gordon could see a white stretched smile of skin. Gordon caught himself, placing his hand securely upon the door as if he might fall back through it otherwise.

The woman was about his age, with a long Irish nose, her complexion roseate and freckled, flushed from the pregnancy. Her eyes were watery blue. Her cornsilk hair had been tied into a makeshift bun, and floating strands escaped around her ears and eyes. She shelved the letters she was holding upon her abdomen as they exchanged looks. Her mouth pursed with expectation, as if Gordon had come specifically to speak to her. But the certainty of her death, the unfairness of its occurring only weeks before her delivery date, crumpled him. He had nothing to tell her. Behind her the fluorescents droned and the envelopes threshed through other hands, sounding like birds flying. Tonight it was the saddest, most resonant thing Gordon had ever heard: the sound of paper being shuffled through the fingers of strangers. She bestowed on him a warm but wistful smile, as if she would rather be somewhere else, and turned her nine-month torso away again, the would-be child inside it gently brushing the workroom counter, possibly placing its tiny fetal toes against the surface through the membrane of her flesh. Long tables and grey conveyors carried language away, away, away.

BACK ON FLOOR TWELVE, Gordon fumbled for the wall switch. He found it, and the squashed room was illuminated by a hollow radiance. He put the key, pilfered from Bentley's podium, into his pocket. The first file he pulled was his own, but soon the stories of others were falling open across his lap.

Rachel: ruptured appendix. Erika: peanut allergy. Jill: crushed in collapsed shopping mall, failure of engineering. Fleur: alcohol poisoning. Fiona: murdered by spouse. Veronica: killed in action. Carma: impaired driving. Manos: death by anaesthesia. Miranda: cancer. Titus: blunt force trauma, suicide suspected. Dave: asthma attack. Chandler: blow to brain, long-term coma, unplugged by family. Gordon: toxification, suicide suspected.

Gordon's own death sounded vaguely familiar to him, as if he were looking out a window he had gazed from every day, this time through a sheer curtain, able to identify the outlines of the trees and roofs even though they were obscured. He could almost recall falling asleep for the last time, the view out the window across from the bed. It was the others that weighed upon him. He rose from the creaking chair, took a few steps, and stood holding the folders, some at the end of each fist, against his pant legs, shoulders pulled down by the pages. Then he folded at the knees, let his backside hit the tiled floor, where he sprawled in the dust, files blanketing him from wrists to shoelaces. He stared at the rows of cabinets before him, drawers crammed with the names — so many names — of those he did not know.

17

HE COULD REMEMBER THE WINDOWS.

The windows had tipped forward, striving toward a trian-gle of wood that pointed upward, a prow, and behind it a ship of glass. The galley was done in redwood, the mates dressed in autumn brown, name-tagged, with vests and headsets — urban sailors in a sea of humans. He recalled with some effort that it was not a ship at all, but a bookstore, a gleaming mega-chain, and he had been outside it looking up.

That seven-dollar-an-hour crew had politely attempted to restrain, impose rules, as they hooked and unhooked chrome-knobbed coils of yellow rope. Chaos, that was their job: to hold back the throng of schoolteachers and nurses, social workers and househusbands, spectacled psychologists and pinstriped grocers, jacketed reviewers and gingham mums with tots in tow. That had been the breadth of Chloe, Gordon told himself, a testament to her, a lineup of absolute love — if not for her herself then for all that she had done. The assemblage wove its way around illuminated pillars and lowboys spread with candlesticks and aromatic pillows, Clancy and Kafka propped up on gravestone-like pedestals, improbably side by side.

From his angle the stairs had been visible, curving round, a spindle of sweaters and coats, of hands clasping the rail and unclasping it, of feet half here and half there, edging their way up with slow eagerness. Desire was audible. The panes conducted it, buzzed with it, with whispers and thrum, so that even there, outside, Gordon had heard the seashell-like roar of an ocean of fans. They were flipping pages of Chloe's first book back and forth, some finding favourite passages, others as-yet-unplumbed depths. In each hand, the same beginning sentence, the same end, the duplication of Chloe's thoughts in the thousands: a tome. A thousand tomes, each with a thousand pages, standing in line.

Past the cappuccino machines on the upper level the figures had wound, pressing on to the prow, where, between the glass panels, Gordon had been able to see her — the Author.

Chloe. She was nodding, her hair like a leaping fire that had been forcibly stapled down to her head by some assistant, some publicist, some well-meaning man-boy in a loose button-up. Gordon recalled thinking that he was permitted only this: her neck, its red-blond stitches, and the curled backs of her ears, just beyond the bow of the book boat. She had floated in a wonky triangle surrounded by sky, or so it had seemed to him then. The occasional black suit had stepped in to add another stack of titles to the diminishing display. It was a new edition of her old book, the one she'd penned with him, dressed up anew — a movie edition with Cate Blanchett on the cover. *Commanding this much attention,* he had marvelled silently where he stood. Beyond the legions of loving faces stretched shelves and shelves of books that Gordon had known would go unread, spines adorned with lesser names, with the slim logos of nearly anonymous publishers, the skeletal works of unloved authors, among them Small: S-M-A-L-L, Gordon.

He had waited for the author to turn and recognize him, knowing with each breath that she wouldn't. That it was over. It had been a full-bright afternoon, the third week of fall — almost eleven years to the day since they first met. Ten years, eleven months, and a week to the day since he had first read her. Gordon had wished then that he could undo it, unlove her. Beyond her, on the same side of the glass as Gordon, a plane had excreted a milky trail across the sky to the right of her temple. She'd closed another book, complete with autograph, and handed it back. As she'd cocked her head to one side, Gordon had thought he saw just the nib of her smile.

Below Chloe, he had stepped from foot to foot, pocketed his hands and then unsheathed them again, knowing exactly what came next. When he had waited long enough, the sun slanted and his reflection was caught between her ankles, tossed back at him. Truthfully, she had probably moved from her station and the ankles were in a backroom with cheerful employees, where she was being poured coffee or wine before signing a few extra copies and saying goodbye. Gordon's eyes and lips were colourless, limp with acidity, like garnish fruit that had been twisted dry.

There had been a pharmacy up a block and across the intersection, right beside the subway's red mouth. Gordon had headed for it, cutting through a covered parking lot, blinking at the sudden dimness, turning his body sideways between cars as if he might set off their alarms by walking too close. Each spot in the vicinity was taken up, presumably by those inside the bookstore, still reluctant to leave. He had stared directly down as he walked; the lines underfoot were neither white nor yellow, Gordon had decided, but the exact colour of bones. A chill had greeted him as he entered the store — central air. He cruised across the ends of the aisles. He had long ago grown accustomed to the Portuguese hanging signs that his neighbourhood *farmacia* favoured. What he was looking for was in English, but it took him longer to find: Sleep-eze, a purple package sprinkled in pinprick stars.

Extra-strength, Gordon had selected. For a second he had held the box in his palm, gazing down at it, enjoying the touch of the cardboard against his skin. He had known that each capsule inside would be wrapped in foil, lying within its own plastic pod. Second thoughts. He had removed another brand from its place. With a flick of his finger it had tucked easily into his other palm. With one in each hand he'd taken both boxes to the young cashier, who was ponytailed and wore a slim cross on her slim neck.

"Are these different? Which of these works better?" He had displayed them, then reluctantly set them before her.

She'd picked up both of his selections and turned them over.

"This one's extra-strength," she'd said. "I guess it depends on your condition." Absently she had placed the boxes back on the counter, a row of lottery tickets encased in a see-through tray beneath them. *Flamingo Bingo. Lucky Gold.*

HEAVEN IS SMALL   175

"I probably shouldn't take more than I really need."

When Gordon had looked up at the cashier again, the small gold cross around her neck had crept its way into her mouth, half under her tongue.

"It might be good to have this one on hand, though, just in case the regular doesn't work." Gordon had felt a grin hardening on his face. His smile fake, he had been certain she would see he was lying.

"Sure," the cashier had said. The gold trinket had bounced back to her chest when she opened her mouth. A droplet of saliva dotted her clavicle. She was looking out the window as she added, "Better safe than sorry." She had dropped his two bright boxes into a white paper bag.

IT WOULD BE WRONG TO CONTINUE to speak in generalities about the past, Gordon typed across his Heaven monitor. Speak to whom? Gordon admitted he was not certain. There were times he believed he was writing into a void, and still others when he was convinced there was indeed some hovering spirit or knowing eye, some Great Creator, present either in or outside the seventy crystal floors of Heaven. But to whomever Gordon was writing, whether it was book-club member Mrs. Mabey in Minnesota, his team of unsuspecting co-workers, the still-living Chloe Gold, or himself alone, he did so because he sensed that the worlds of the dead and the living were not that far apart.

After all, Gordon had arrived by public transit, or at the very least some dream of public transit, something far more

fathomable than the route of birth itself. The idea that somehow he and Heaven's staff could shuttle missives — and even
fully produced romance novels, complete with sales reports
— back and forth between the living and the dead, whether
by post, fax, e-mail, or some system of faith, seemed to
Gordon as believable as anything else he had encountered in
his short time on Planet Earth. Consequently, these were the
dynamics Gordon played with in his very loose "fiction" (so
loose even Gordon imagined it inside a large set of finger
quotes). This fiction involved a hero named Graham and a
heroine named Zoe.

> To find myself here, in this place, writing this,
> seems as plausible as the fact that my name is
> Graham and I topped at five feet ten after arriving in
> the world at a mere eighteen inches. That I should
> have been born on this continent and not one of the
> other six. That by the age of twelve I discovered, like
> so many who went before me, that a part of my
> anatomy could suddenly double in size in the pres-
> ence of the feminine form — amazing! That my heart
> was the size of a fist but felt like a watermelon for the
> first two-thirds of my life, only to shrink down to a
> grape seed one day. That any woman, let alone Zoe,
> deigned to love me — love with the whole soul —
> deigned to think of me at all, to call me and wait for
> me, to want to hold my surely reptilian hand, let
> alone hold me upon her sinuous tongue inside her
> mouth's arching cathedral.

As believable as the fact that Zoe went for me hook, line, and sinker, leaving me messages and, when — to my own surprise — I didn't call back, leaving me more. That it took us two months to be alone together for more than our first rushed half-hour of small talk. That when we finally did connect, she fed me cappuccinos until I shook, and then we lay very still — or as still as possible, given my jitters — in her bed together, she in a pair of long johns and me in my T-shirt and boxer shorts. That we spooned as tentative snow fell outside her window on a tree that looked like it had been scythed clear down the middle. That a shellac of sleep dampened her skin and I climbed into each breath she offered and stretched out inside it. That we slept this way — or lay without sleep in my case, as I counted each glimmering flake beneath the streetlight — for three consecutive nights before I finally had the guts to sweep her hair aside and place another kiss across her neck. That she turned to face me and disposed of my T-shirt and boxers with a ferocity that chilled and, at the same time, fevered me. That she left small marks up to my ears, biting and nipping at my jaw and not letting go, even when I grabbed her by the wrists and pushed her away in pain. That this was before serenity took over her life, before the driftwood and the semi-precious stones, the herbs and pennyroyal teas, the chunks of crystal, the incense sticks and candles, the seashells like old bones lining the windowsills.

That there were days when she invited me out to galleries and introduced me to other young men, who painted themselves blue or wore lipstick and eyeliner or dyed their manes candy-floss pink, who pierced their tongues, who wrote letters to institutionalized serial killers, or who were working on stage adaptations of Leonard Cohen's *Beautiful Losers*. That Zoe would once do anything for a kick, for attention. That she was Zoe of the turquoise toenails, and, like all the henna girls, vainly ironed her naturally red-and-curly to hang down her back. That she took to wearing the masks of *bonheur* and *tristesse* on her fingers in sterling silver, and drove reckless and drunk sometimes, and would phone me late at night playing needy games on the other end of the line. That she and I married at all, let alone dated. That there was a justice of the peace quoting Langston Hughes, and Zoe's younger sister as witness, and a video that zoomed in on the $3.99 daisies I had bought on our mad dash there — because Zoe was always late — from a woman on the main street with a blanket and a black plastic bucket and no teeth. That I do, you see, remember it after all, in moments when I'm not looking. That in the first year in our house there was unkempt passion that now I only read about.

That, like the Aries she was, she controlled our Saturdays and Sundays and every spare weekday minute with her plans, plans, plans. That she had this need to control. That it was wondrous and savage and gave shape to my otherwise aimless, head-bobbing life. That I occasionally railed against her for the fun of it, playing the devil's advocate to see how she would twist her own arguments to be right. That there was a certain way to salt eggs. That there was a specific time to take out the recycling at night. That we so often collided mid-argument, and found each other's mouths. That Zoe's mouth had no end. That she was exultant when naked and oftentimes crass, ecstatic, forceful, frivolous, or full of fart jokes, difficult to pin down but always there, and wholly so, eager for everything that came her way. That she would turn around afterward, defensively, and claim I had no idea — no idea at all — what to do with a woman. That her mouth was still there, again, again, and again.

That the changes occurred first in her writing. That while I was there staring at the great blank carrige of the typewriter that sat in a makeshift corner of our living room, I could hear Zoe's fingers snapping over the keys in the room she insisted be all her own, her ancient computer groaning through the walls whenever she hit Control + S, which was often. That what began as a poem, "Ode to Amethyst Light," sprinkled with borrowed terms from meteorology, could blow easy-breezy into a series of poems, and then one book-length prose poem, and then an actual, bona fide novel, with seemingly no effort at

all. That she became, finally, a calm person, a sophisticated, patient person I didn't know, one who medi-
tated or went for walks when she was irked with me,
when she "needed to understand" me better, this person who wasn't looking for scandal or accolades or
instant satisfaction any more, but was more concerned with what she was making happen on an illuminated square just a foot or two outside of her head
— a strange, solitary sphere entirely different from
her hedonistic world.

That in only thirteen or fourteen months she
became a person who claimed she had supported me,
who claimed it was my turn to support her in her
writing career. That she was right, without making a
pretzel of the argument. And worse, that it stung
dreadfully.

That I sent out a bad first draft of a second novel,
and confided to Zoe, and my old roommate, and
Susan and Janey, and Zoe's beautiful gang of misfits,
and anyone who would listen, that I was sure it would
be accepted anyway, "given the state of publishing."
That I went drinking — yes, I did — for the entire
twelve months it took for the manuscript, and the
rejection notice, to come back to me. That the notice
was not even on letterhead, but on a quarter-cut scrap
of paper bearing an over-inked wood stamp (purple)
with the publisher's mailing address, as if some intern
had printed off the slips in bulk, four to a page to save
on paper, and cut them apart with scissors and

stamped them for me and the other losers. That the
message read: *Dear Author, thank you for your submission.
Unfortunately, it is not right for our publishing house at this
time. We wish you the best of luck in placing it elsewhere.
Please do not contact us for comments; regrettably, our sched-
ules do not allow us the time to make individual assessments.
Best wishes, The Editors.* That, because I had published
my first novel with this house, the editor — singular
— took the time to scrawl in blue pen on the back:
Thanks, Graham. Sorry, maybe the next one. That the slip
of paper inscribed with so much weight, so much
heartbreak and rejection, was the size of a grade-
school valentine and held on by a lone blue paper clip.
That I felt it clipped to my throat before my eyes had
even scanned the generic *thanks/no thanks.*

That I called up the editor and told him I understood completely, one hundred percent, that I had
known it wasn't quite there yet but that I was rework-
ing it and would you like to see it again, and no, no,
that was fine too, no hard feelings, sure we'll get a
beer sometime, and that's all right anyway because
there was this great little press I had just heard about
in Wisconsin and maybe I would try there, and could
I use your name in the letter, and thank you, thanks,
thanks so much, and sure I'd tell Zoe you said hi, and
yes, she *was* working on something, and yes it *was* a
novel, but no, it wasn't ready yet, and likely it wouldn't
be for a very long time, if at all, well, you know
Zoe, but sure, of course, of course, I would remember

to tell her to tell you more about it, and okay, well then, and guess that's goodbye ...

That during this time, when I came into the room, Zoe would hold up her finger, lick her lips, eyes dancing across the monitor before her, both monitor and eyes glowing green, green, and greener still in the fast-darkening house. That in the end, she — an English dropout peddling cantaloupe-coloured skirts at The Limited, although she wouldn't shop anywhere but the Salvation Army — went on to write the kind of beach volume she disdained. That it was an eight-hundred-page best-selling novel in which the, ahem, wind took on the soul of the protagonist's dead grandmother and related their entire family history across three generations, all within a few moments in the protagonist's greatest hour of need.

That the boxes, labelled *Author*, arrived the day before Zoe was to move out. That it was 8:30 a.m. when the doorbell rang. That I was half-naked, hungover, throat still dry as Styrofoam chips. That I had puked ouzo only a couple of hours before and was now standing in my homeliest pair of boxers, the ones that were ripped at the waistband. That I was cursing the refrigerator because it failed to contain a carton of milk, and staring into a bath of black coffee that smelled like the Detroit River after spring thaw. That when the knock came, echoing through the half-packed-up duplex, Zoe peered out the window, saw the courier's truck, and jerked open the door with a big *whoosh*, in spite of our attire, letting the March air stiffen her nipples beneath the unbleached tank top that she wore to bed. That I knew this, even from behind her in the kitchen, where I danced on the cold tiles and hid my abhorrent, scrawny, hairy, boxered self behind the fridge door, yelling "Zoe!" and subjecting myself to further shrinkage. That the delivery person was not a man but a woman, with a close-cropped orange scalp not unlike Zoe's own (recently), who looked as though she could have been Zoe's big brother/sister, especially as she held the box atop her shoulder while presenting Zoe with an electric clipboard, a pen-shaped object, and several unhidden glances from Zoe's neck down to her Chinese slippers as Zoe fumbled with her own name.

That Zoe said, "It's my novel!" revolving between me and Annie Lennox as though we should both be thrilled on her behalf. That the woman said, "That so?" and "Congratulations!" That I said nothing. That I wouldn't come out from behind the refrigerator door until the courier had gone, and then I saw that I had spilled coffee down the side of one boxer leg, and the garment was sodden and clung to me, emphasizing the way my balls had curled up like a pair of baby piglets.

That she opened the box in front of me and sighed, peeling the luscious aquamarine matte jacket off to see her name — Zoe Silver, she had decided just before it went to print, not Zoe Silver-Little — embossed on the everlasting black cloth spine.

That my eye should catch on the first word of the title as she redressed her work: *Goodbye*. That as she was folding the silky dust jacket around the book again, a stitch of fatigue, frustration, or uncertainty appeared on Zoe's forehead above the bridge of her nose, a shape like a scallop, and she turned the thing over, then back, then dropped it into the box with the others, like it didn't mean a thing. That the tome landed with a resounding, unforgettable *thud*. That I continue to hear this sound even now, in that moment when I am just about to fall asleep. That, like a lucid dream, I feel myself falling and the book falling instantly in my mind, the two at the same time, *thud* — for seven years, *thud* and *thud* and a thousand *thud*s, and even after death, it seems, this sound, this *thud*, unlike the other *ka-thunk*s and *ker-plunk*s that exist in the universe — will jerk me bolt upright, clutching at the bedclothes, or, if I'm sitting upright already, as I do at work, the arms of my chair.

Gordon leaned back in his chair and ran his eyes over what he had written. He had composed nine pages of sentence fragments, but the question of grammar was less important to him than whether the content itself would fly. He wiped a hand down his face, erasing his expression and preparing for what came next. Given that everything in his life had been possible, it did seem to Gordon that his continued existence after death was real — as real as anything else. And under the glow of Heaven's fluorescents it was easy to believe in contact between the worlds. The light fixtures poured a tranquil, humming liquor over his head.

A hundred more pages, Daves had said. That was in addition to what he'd already written. If it was to meet their purposes it had to add up to almost two hundred pages in layout. Gordon's lips welded around his pen. Bouncing it up and down with his tongue, the Paper Mate became a conductor's baton as Gordon began typing again, fingers gaining momentum. He did not know whether the screen remained blank or was filling with words as steadily as rain coming in through a carelessly raised window at night in a bedroom now long gone. He did not know whether his fingers were moving or whether God or magnetics moved them for him. He was like a boy with a wobbly Ouija board in his lap, consumed by near-carnal exhilaration and trepidation. Gordon's pale, furred knuckles trembled over letters. He did not type so much as feel an unconscious swelling of music that made itself into a membrane between himself and the illuminated offices in which he sat, alone. The trembling black tongue of the pen extended from his lips, a strange snake. His shapeless hair had been tugged up unconsciously in the back. His eyes, sombre and devious, darted back and forth.

Now he was not bent over a desk at all but lying in grass, the smell of mud stuck up his nostrils; he was throat-deep in the astringent perfumes of women, from the talc of the first squeaky-voiced girl he had danced with in high school to the lime-laced breath of Chloe's thighs. Or he was running, the concrete of urban streets reverberating in his kneecaps and his skeletal rib cage, the yellow splintered street lights of youth swinging on cabled breaths. What crept into being were the anthills of chapters.

The pen travelled from right mouth corner to left mouth corner, assumed an erect stance, a flaccid position, and eventually dropped from his lips into his lap, only to be collected again in a moment of inspiration as someone in the Design Department cruised in early and set about shredding the night with the push of a button and the whirr of a scanner drum. All night Gordon had followed himself from birth to Heaven, documenting everything he could remember, no matter how translucent or vague. When he couldn't remember, he tore the roofs off the apartments in which he had lived and let the walls and flotsam-jetsam possessions remain true, floating amid the fakery, added men and women to the rooms like small effigies and moved them about among his furnishings, until their plastic faces felt somehow better than the truth. And when that seemed not to work, he resorted to his favourite method — random lists.

The things Gordon found he remembered most clearly were not his living moments but his dreaming ones. He had never been one who dreamed. That was Chloe territory. Still he could hear her recounting her own sagas, until they became in his memory a single endless dream:

"I dreamt that you were a zebra and I was a mouse ..."

"We were stuck in the middle of the French Revolution ..."

"I was explaining various sex toys to my mother ..."

"I dreamt my aunt edited my *Complete Works of Chaucer* textbook ..."

"We went to a party but I was wearing only these godawful underpants ..."

"We tried to escape but it started to snow . . ."

"Then I was dating an actor . . ."

"You were sitting in a bathtub with your clothes on, but you had no legs, only an empty pair of pants . . ."

"I was in a schoolbus with my little sister and it was filling up with water . . ."

"I was in The Limited storeroom again . . ."

"I lay down at work and watched all of the workplace continue around me from the vantage point of the carpet . . ."

Gordon had always denied to Chloe that he had dreams; he claimed he forgot them the instant he opened his eyes. But now they came floating back to him, the way they occasionally had in that second when he lay back down at night. At Heaven the dreams seemed more vivid, and the characters who peopled them as real as any Gordon had actually met during his life.

He recalled other odd things as well. Small moments that had occurred while he was alive now seemed to stretch out and weigh more heavily. For example, a woman he had once passed on the subway car. She had stepped off as he was getting on; there had been an uncanny familiarity to her, as if she was a long-lost cousin or a kindergarten classmate now grown. At the same time Gordon had been certain he had never seen her before. They had both turned back and she had opened her mouth as if to speak before the doors clunked closed between them. Things like that. Or the time about six months after the publication of Chloe's first book: coincidentally they had been riding at opposite ends of the same crowded subway car. Gordon had caught a glimpse of Chloe's head from behind, one of her thumbs wrapping the pole, her sandals peeking out among the corduroy, blue jeans, and houndstooth. Although he had never seen this particular pair of sandals before, Gordon had been certain they were Chloe's, as were the feet inside them, not to mention that thumb — hers, with its trim white cuticle. His heart hung on his tongue. Would she see him? Would they speak, they who had lived and slept and showered together? He had been paralyzed by the prospect. When the crowd shifted, sandals and hair were blocked. Then there had been only that one digit within his view, still holding on, and he had known it as hers from fifty feet away. Even in his panic he loved the thumb so much he had ridden three extra stops to continue memorizing it — and he never spoke of the moment to anyone. All of these things Gordon now documented.

THE NEXT DAY, at his desk in Cubicle 133 of Floor Twelve, Heaven, he could not remember what he had written the night before. When Gordon flipped the computer from DOS mode to Windows, abandoning a dozen suitors and fumbled snoggings, he was cock-a-hoop to see that indeed he had written *something*, that one might call it writing of a sort. There were paragraphs, full pages, chapters. The pen bounced up hard. Gordon skimmed the virtual pages, still too afraid to print them out but congratulated nonetheless by the phrases enclosed in their white perimeters: a welcoming (he thought) snatch of dialogue, and the delightfully rancorous cigarettes, teacups, and national holidays of any American short story. Phrases flashed out at him like grinning men in worn brown suits.

Gordon pressed his fingers to his temples and attempted to mentally retrieve the pages of the second-hand paperbacks that had lined his shelves for years, both the thumbed ones and those bought but barely consumed. He attempted to reference them from a distance or crib their cadence. There was a line he still remembered from a John Berryman poem: *All my love, my falsity, my anti-hopes.* And so, over the course of a few nights, slipping between fiction and memoir, Gordon worked an account of his life into one long letter to earnest book-club member Mrs. Abigail Mabey in Minnesota, and whoever else might read it.

To scroll was a thing like God. To send the final file to Daves was even better. Gordon prepared the e-mail and clicked Send.

18

A MANILA ENVELOPE LAY ON TOP OF GORDON'S INBOX.

It was too soon to have received anything back about his and Daves' book. Off it had gone just last week. Too afraid to print out the proof, Daves had called Gordon into his office to show him the final layout onscreen. "It's all you now, Gordo," Daves had said, indicating that the original book's text had been completely knocked out and replaced by Gordon's. A title and an author name still clung to the cover, but the love story inside was no romance. Gordon had nodded and Daves had sent it off to the Print Division downstairs, a purple progress bar filling in slowly — 8%, 30%, 55%, 82%, 90%, 99%, 100% — as the file transferred. When Gordon had asked how long until it reached its audience, Daves had shrugged in his usual manner, plaid shoulders twitching as if shaking off snow. "It's more like newspaper or magazine publishing than book publishing. It's a matter of weeks or days, not months or years," Daves had answered calmly. "But I can't imagine we'll hear anything until after Christmas-slash-Hanukkah."

With shaking hands Gordon reached for his inbox, tore open the package, and held the second non-Heaven title to reach him from the other side. He thumbed it open. There it was. His poem. In print. Selected from one of the packages he had sent out to literary journals the day he first saw the mailroom. It was the only one he had submitted that wasn't a love poem.

To: From:
Gordon Small

Jesus e-mailed me this morning
and his subject line was: *What?*

I thought he must have heard me,
calling his name in the night

when I had been abandoned,
when the filaments rattled

like small stones inside the lights,
when the waiting walls raised moss —

But it seemed what he wanted
was to sell me a new watch.

Gordon Small works in a cubicle at Heaven Books. He is pretty sure he is already dead. Previously he released a novella entitled The Mercy Seat. *This is his first published poem.*

Gordon felt a current of heat creep over his face. He shut the magazine. He rolled open his top drawer, dropped the volume in. He looked at the magazine inside the drawer. The cover had a face pencilled in blue inside a small square. It was neither a man's nor a woman's face. Behind the blue face, colour leaked through. Red streaks, like someone had bled on the man (or woman) or, more accurately, bled somewhere behind him (or her). Gordon let the drawer snap back on its springs. The cover with his poem behind it disappeared into a flat façade of wood grain.

It was a stupid poem.

Gordon tossed the magazine envelope into his recycling bin and turned on his computer. He waited for it to load. Icons took their place along the bottom of his screen. A purple happy face with a line splitting it in two popped up. Gordon waited for the face to go away. When it had, he logged on to the Heaven system and entered the code for his next assigned romance novel. *Carousel of Dreams* appeared at the top of the illuminated text. Gordon edged the cursor down the page. Though the books Heaven published had no page breaks until they went to Daves, Gordon still considered the screen he viewed as a page, an endless page. One page that led to the end of the book, the last line, the end of the story. The place where the story ran out of words. Gordon scrolled through what might have been four pages, though of course he couldn't say. At line 127 he began to lean his chin on one hand.

Gordon pulled open the drawer. The blue face stared up at him with translucent pastel eyes. Beneath it he found the poem again. He reread the revealing biographical note first, guessing it had been shrugged off by the editorial committee as whacky writer humour rather than an actual communiqué from the other side. He reread the poem. The filaments. He could live with the filaments. It was only the poem's closing line, really, that turned it into a joke. A one-liner. Har-dee-har-har. A-fat-man-with-a-cigar kind of a poem. He wondered if Chloe's *post–* poem had really been as good as he had thought at the time. Maybe he had only thought so to convince himself he was selecting important things. He wondered if Chloe had felt like he did now. He wondered why he himself had been so confident, long ago, about his own brief fiction.

Gordon dropped the magazine into the drawer. He bit one thumb as if his own poem had given him a paper-cut. He kneed the drawer closed and the publication credit fell back into wooden invisibility.

He was scrolling through Chapter Four when the drawer popped open. Gordon was sure he hadn't touched it. But there it was, springing wide of its own accord. Gordon eyed the magazine warily. The man/woman blue-eyed him back side-long, the expression of the lips unchanging: slightly down-turned, but definitely not a full frown. Gordon picked up the literary journal. *Literary.* The word filled his mind with a sugary euphoria. He flipped quickly to page 44.

It was a good poem after all. *Gordon Small. To: From. Small, Gordon. From: To.*

"Gordon Small . . ."

It took a moment for him to realize the voice wasn't in his head.

"*Gordon?*" Chandler, who seldom made her way through

the cubicles, flapped a blurred sheet of paper at him over the partition. Gordon made a mouselike sound in his throat and scrambled to conceal the magazine within the desk drawer once again. In true Chandler fashion she leaned nimbly but urgently into his cubicle, the smell of Lancôme's Poême accompanying her. He bet the whole neighbourhood where she had lived on Earth smelled of skin cream.

"Have you *seen* this?!" she whisper-shrieked, shaking a Xerox in his face. It was too close for him to make out.

Why did Chandler *emphasize* everything she said? Gordon imagined an angel perched on her shoulder with a fat high-lighter, illuminating the morphemes as they fell from her lips. She was practically shivering with excitement — the way she did when she had gossip to convey.

She let the page fall between them.

Gordon ducked his head, his mouth hitting his shirt collar as he read. "Oh, fuddle-duddle," he muttered. Then, louder, the word released as he'd intended. "Oh. Oh . . . fuck."

The blurred ink read: "CHLOE GOLD TO CHAMPION UNKNOWN AUTHOR."

Gordon's hands started to shake as he strained to read what appeared to be a newspaper article that had been clipped, then copied from a previous photocopy, degenerating in the process:

CHLOE GOLD TO CHAMPION UNKNOWN AUTHOR
"I will conduct a worldwide search for this author, whoever he or she may be," novelist Chloe Gold stated in a press conference on Monday. Gold referred to a mysterious and utterly anonymous writer who came

to her attention after she found a brief notice about the prankster on Booktroll, a blog popular with those in literary publishing.

Gold claims she will "employ as many hands and minds as needed to uncover the text's true author," whom she hopes to champion. "What we have here is an absolute reverse of the J.T. Leroy situation. I went out and found the paperback Booktroll referenced. Immediately I felt as if I were reading a story that had been written just for me," Gold closed with emotion after admitting the book had left her "flabbergasted." Gold's own resumé boasts the award-winning *Goodbye to the Wind* and the new and lauded *Hello Twilight*.

According to Booktroll, the author-at-large seems to have sneaked his or her own writing into the world inside the covers of someone else's novel. According to Gold, "There has never been an unhappy romance. Never has any novel in the romance genre, introduced through Heaven Books or by one of its competitors, touched upon the topics of alcoholism, abortion, divorce, lesbian relationships, or suicide. Never have the hero and heroine parted ways or come to violent ends." All of that changed when an author writing under the name Allison Sharpe offered Heaven readers a heart-rending incomplete love story in the form of a letter addressing an actual book-club member, Abigail Mabey.

Reporters were quick to reach Mabey by phone at her home in St. Paul, Minnesota. She confirmed that she received the book by mail through Heaven's Sealed-with-a-Kiss Club but has not yet read it. "I certainly intend to," she said.

Heaven Books author Allison Sharpe has three previous titles with the company. The real Sharpe says she did have a book called *Darling Deception* under contract, but the title as it has been released "contains not a single bloody word" from her pen.

Covered in the standard lavender script of Heaven's Secret Hearts imprint, a love-meets-suspense line, the text itself may be what its title, *Darling Deception*, declares. Bloggers have been debating whether the book is a publishing mix-up or if it marks a bold new direction for romance publishing. Some posit this title may have been a market test. The company has previously said it plans to introduce new fiction lines to reflect more contemporary dating trends.

At the time of printing, messages left for the publisher were not being returned.

If Gordon could have burst into a cold sweat, he would have. Unconsciously he placed a hand upon his forehead and slowly mopped it over his brow. "Have you showed it to Daves?"

"Dave? In Layout?" Chandler still hadn't wrapped her head around Daves' plural name. "Why would I show him?"

Eyes rescanning the flecked photocopy, Gordon continued to blurt out questions. "Where did you get this? Is it going around? Why didn't I hear about this from Ivy up in the Net Division?"

Chandler leaned a hip against his desk and blinked her long lashes, finally having found Gordon's eyes with hers again. "Because, darling . . ." One amused finger reached out and squiggled its way down between his pecs. It sent shivers through his knock-kneed body. Chandler's irises were full of a coy green light. She got to the end of his tie and flipped it mockingly into his face, her finger breaking away just before the exchange reached obscenity. "You're hearing it from *me*. As department head, don't I always have the best scoops? Don't I always know what's what?"

Before Gordon could react, Chandler turned and exited his cramped quarters. "By the way," she called back over her shoulder, "you're wanted upstairs."

Gordon stood and put a hand to his chest, where a tiny maraca shook, the antidepressants quivering along with the rest of him.

"Ms. Lillian Payne in HR asked me to send you up for a meeting. 'Immediately,' she said." Chandler invested *immediately* with her most professional tone. She winked as she rounded the corner and disappeared.

Gordon stood inside his suit. In his suit, inside his cubicle, Gordon stood. He stood, blinking with the shock of Chandler's mock invitation and the very real fact that he was being called up to Floor Seventy for the first time since he had been interviewed. As he stood he imagined that if Daves were to come out of his production office and see Gordon standing there, hands limp at his sides, from that far perspective Daves would confront a series of pink walls leading to other nooks where computers and people-like people sat, and at the end of them all would be Gordon, centred between the dividers of his world. A man of moderate height and moderate build, in olive-coloured armour against a backdrop of pink wool and pink tin shelving. If one of the men from the Design Department were to glance over, that man would see the five-foot-ten Gordon staring, standing, staring, standing, staring. The man in his suit. The man inside a romance factory. The man full of fear. The small man.

It took Gordon a few moments to realize what he was waiting for. Heartbeat. Adrenalin. As foolish as such things were to wait for, he found he missed them terribly.

Gordon cleared his throat. No one looked over from Design. No one came out of the production office. Over the partition wall he could hear Jill talking on the phone to her sister — or at her, or some idea of her: "You wouldn't believe the amount of calcium contained in sesame."

Jill had a habit of calling people up and offering them advice for which they — likely — hadn't asked. Today she was explaining why eating sesame seeds would absolutely save her sister's cuticles.

"Buy a package for your spice rack. You can sprinkle those bad boys on salads, chicken, add it to your granola in the morning, you name it."

It was an ordinary day in Heaven.

Gordon cleared his throat again. He coughed. He put four fingers over his voice box and felt it. To no one in particular he said, "Hello . . .

"Hello. My name is Gordon Small."

He continued to stand, blinking, in his cubicle, wearing a

concentrating face. Presently he flicked open the exploited drawer. He removed and tossed aside the literary journal, which flipped up on its square-bound spine. Beneath it was a sea of uncapped stick pens. Gordon selected one, scrawled on a Post-it to ensure that the pen had not gone dry, recorded his message, slapped the note onto his computer monitor, put the pen in his jacket pocket, and left his cubicle.

The monitor shone through the melon-hued Post-it, illuminating a fast-scrawled spiral and a phone number without a name. As the computer fell to sleep, the screensaver moon rose around the edges of the sticky.

PART IV

JANUARY

19

THERE WERE 10,775 EMPLOYEES working in the Heaven Book Corporation Building. Lillian Payne reminded herself of this fact as she sat staring at her e-mail inbox. Sixty-four messages sat stacked upon one another: Google Alert after Google Alert. In the past two days they had gone from a couple to a crowd, and the brouhaha had only just begun. Instinctively Lillian knew this, in spite of the Head Office directive that she hold steady and wait to see if the hubbub would fizzle out of its own accord, as so many online scandals did, playing out briefly among a few devoted conspiracy theorists. Lillian drew her shoulders up to her ears, then let them fall again. When she did, she had made her decision. The troublemakers in the company — all and any — would need to be rounded up and questioned. Blogs and message boards were buzzing, and now an actual print article was circulating on the sly around *her* office building, not to mention the sixty-four alerts in her inbox. It was time.

In the top right corner window on the screen, a woman's head sprang up like an orange tulip from the surrounding snowlike drifts of paper. Her hand reached out and raised the receiver on her desk to her ear at the same moment that her voice crawled into Lillian's.

"I need to see Gordon Small. Send him up to HR," Lillian commanded after returning the woman's greeting. Lillian looked down at a pile of manila folders, already thumbing past Small's to the others. "Can you spare him? . . . Yes, now . . . Excellent." The receiver fell back into its cradle and Lillian rose, approached the immense monitor. She watched a strange dance of flirtation and self-consciousness occur between her two employees in the quarter-cut window. In their respective televised sections Workman, E., Fast, J., and Bauer, V., remained hunched before their computers, nothing changing but their finger positions as they scrolled, typed, or plucked M&Ms from dishes on their desks and transported them to mouths that existed beneath the crowns in Lillian's view.

Onscreen, in the lower section of the Editorial 12-I window, Small, G., and Goods, C., tap danced around a sheet of paper — their shapes merging briefly — then parted ways. Lillian's news obviously delivered, a squat green figure was left alone on the edge of the screen. Lillian leaned forward, peering at the top of Small's dishevelled head. She counted the beats of his immobility with her metronome tongue. An odd nausea expanded inside her.

Utterly illogical, she told herself. Physicality was an illusion. She twisted at the waist until her straight, dancer's shoulders were at right angles to her hips. Then she uncoiled and stretched in the other direction.

She glanced at the LCD screen: the man still had not made a move toward their appointment.

Lillian had neither eaten nor drunk a thing in decades. Even though she knew it meant nothing to anyone else, she prided herself on her restraint, her ability to shake off the routines of mortals. She liked to keep a fresh cup of coffee on her desk, though, which she moved around like a fragrant paperweight, particularly when others were present. When she saw the physical pause that resulted from her directive to Small, G. — he had passed, finally, from one onscreen window into another — she left her office and retrieved a newly wetted mug, which she held securely in both hands and contemplated.

Lillian lowered her head and let her lip trail its dark line, but didn't drink. It was the closest she had come in years. There were plenty of discontented employees, she told herself. Of the 10,774 (not including herself) she could think of at least 500 who might engage in low-level sabotage. Small's wife was mentioned in the article, and it would be a strange twist of fate indeed if the man were entirely innocent. Still, she had not achieved her advanced position by venturing guesses or taking haphazard actions. When Lillian looked up, Small's shape was emerging from the elevator on her floor. She rose and closed the doors of the cabinet that housed the LCD screen, the coffee mug handle still floating in her hand as she rounded her desk and found the knob of her office door.

"Come in," she said to Small's blinking visage. He clearly had not expected her to anticipate his arrival so accurately. They were always blinking. *Why do they blink so much when they have no reason?* she never ceased to wonder. She turned her back to Small, G. Human habit was still one of the great mysteries to her. The power of addiction appalled and fascinated. "Do you know why you're here?"

Small, G., took this in the philosophical sense; when Lillian turned back around, she could see that he did. She reminded herself to choose her words carefully. She watched him fold at the knees into a waiting chair he had not yet been offered. She set her cup upon the tidy surface of her desk with a resolute and satisfying *clunk*, and remained on her feet for just a second longer before lowering herself to his level.

The two of them sat examining each other for a moment. Small, G., was definitely worried. His eyes scrunched at the corners and one eyebrow twitched. He resembled an oversized, slightly blind mouse. It was not how she remembered him from the interview. He had been high-strung then, but not lacking in charm. A wonder, really, considering the circumstances of his death.

"Am I under review?" he now peeped.

She slid the folder from the side of her desk to the centre and folded her hands schoolteacher-style upon it. She closed her eyes. When she reopened them, she said slowly, "We are *all* under review."

"But my work — my work performance," Small, G., stuttered. "Is — is there a problem?"

"Perhaps." Lillian opened the file on her desk. There were the co-worker complaints. People grew tired of sitting next to one another; many good employees at Heaven had had complaints filed against them. When she had assumed her role in

HR, making the shift from the lower levels, there had been a folder of unfavourable charges as thick as her thumb. Lillian took her time leafing silently through the complaints, letting Small, G., shift in his chair while she picked up her pencil and quickly marked a column of boxes that fell in the middle of the sheet — 3s on a scale of 1 to 5. She put little faith in complaints.

Finally, having decided the trail of reason she would follow, Lillian reached out and laid a finger on the mug on her desk, as though it were a touchstone. It was a piece of Heaven branding from the 1980s, a row of hearts in mauve, mint, banana, and sea blue. H-e-a-v-e-n wound around the rim in cursive. She had always been rather fond of it. "Do you consider a complaint of sexual harassment to be a problem?"

"I don't understand."

Rather than meeting her straight-ahead gaze, Small's eyes fixed on the folder, which had his name on it written in reverse order — the way Lillian preferred to identify all her employees. It was accurate, and it kept her alert.

"A serious formal complaint has been lodged against you. Whether or not you consider that to be a problem I don't know," Lillian replied, opening the folder. "Mr. J. Manos — your direct superior — reported that he did not know if you were making an invitation to him or issuing a threat . . ."

Small, G., said nothing.

Lillian continued evenly, "You instructed him to stand at the sinks in the men's room and listen carefully while washing his hands?"

Still Small, G., gave no answer but merely sat blinking. Lillian wondered if this meeting would indeed be easier than she'd expected. She began to relax a little. She laid the paper down. "The implication, he felt, was that you might be lurking in the stall in a predatory manner."

Small's face shifted visibly, his eyebrows engaging in a two-step with each other.

"Yes or no, is this what you said to Mr. Jonathan Manos?"

Small, G., moved uncomfortably. "Yes . . . but the scenarios he is implying were not my intention."

Lillian selected a pen and began to write. "'Not Mr. Small's intention.' Was the conversation work-related?"

"In a manner."

"What manner?"

"What are the consequences of this complaint?" Small, G., dodged.

"The consequences" — Lillian set down the pen, lowered her eyes — "are inconsequential providing there are no further complaints."

"But . . . ?"

There. This was what she had anticipated.

"But," Lillian acknowledged, tilting her head to one side and leafing through a stack of papers, "there *have* been other complaints."

Small, G., nodded.

"Suddenly, Mr. Small, you don't seem too surprised. Why is that?" She fixed him with what she knew to be her cold-sweat glare.

In response, Small, G., wound his hands around the armrests. "The question I asked Mr. Manos was of a personal nature," he admitted, staring up at her. She saw that his jaw was now locked with resolve. "But the conversation was also work-related. It was regarding the personal habits of my co-workers, a question that was worrying me and impeding my ability to do my job. It is difficult, you must admit," Small, G., elaborated, "to do your job well if you feel your own habits or behaviours are not in step with those around you. The number of acceptable bathroom breaks, for instance . . ." His voice trailed off.

Lillian made a note.

"If I may ask, what —" Small, G., leaned forward. "What are the other complaints?"

"You tell me, Mr. Small."

Nothing.

Lillian turned the page. "A Ms. Fiona Christiansen detailed a rather unusual choice of birthday card that you had given her. Did you give her a birthday card?"

Small, G., nodded.

She quickly moved on. "Fleur and Carma insisted that you continued to leave the same messages every day even though each confirmed receipt of said messages and asked you to desist, and a Ms. Erika Workman is convinced, based on your musical tastes, that you want to kill her."

There was a pause, during which Small, G., gripped the armrests more fiercely.

"You are not denying these actions, then?"

"I think Erika should not read too much into popular music. I —" The man stuttered and glanced away from Lillian. "I am very absent-minded. Especially when I have been working hard."

Lillian sat up straighter and leafed through the file before her. Although she did not believe in feelings, a feeling had been growing inside her. She could sense its vague presence rearranging her stomach, her uterus, pushing against her bladder and bowels. Even the base of her spine. It had been so long since she had had the opportunity to process a feeling of her own that she was not entirely sure which one it was — endangerment or bemusement? So she sat up straighter and plunged on. "According to your time sheets, your productivity is down, and in the short time you've been at Heaven Books, you've been written up once already for carelessness. But yes, I am aware of your tendency to stay on at your desk quite late into the evening."

"Where should I go?"

Lillian put the papers down. For a moment she found herself indexing all that she had said and done in an effort to comprehend how Small, G., had arrived at such a simple, direct, disruptive question. She said nothing, letting her next move form in her mind. Then, "Frankly, Mr. Small, that is not my concern." It came out with a slight smile, even as the strange and solid feeling inside her crackled, gaped like breaking ice. "I have a copy of your contract here. This is your signature?" She slid the papers toward him.

Small, G., tugged at them eagerly and stared so long at the papers she suspected he was reading the document in its entirety, including its finest print.

"You agree here" — she gestured, for the sake of efficiency — "to be present between the hours of nine and five-thirty, five days per week. And here you agree that you do not have privileges to access any floor that is not your own, nor to remain in your cubicle nor in the areas of the gym, cafeteria, nor lobby beyond the hours of six at night nor before the hour of eight in the morning, nor on any weekend, without express consent from your supervisor, department head, or from HR."

"So where should I go?" the man in the green suit repeated, firmly but quietly. To Lillian's ears his voice carried a terrible earnestness.

"It is my experience," she advised him, "that finding one's way to one's car is the standard response to the end of the working day."

"I don't own a car."

"You have heard of carpooling? Millions of North Americans —" she began.

"Are we —"

Something about his expression cut Lillian short, against her better judgement.

"Are we even *in* North America?"

Lillian chose to ignore the question. "Look . . . Gordon," she said, using his name for the first time since she'd admitted him to Heaven, "it's like this. When you were a child, you didn't question recess. Certainly you *could* have stayed indoors and played Tonka truck on the floor tiles, or gone to the gym or to the library, but you *didn't*. The teacher preferred that you played outside, so out you went, and you didn't question why, even when it was raining. Those were the rules. There are rules here too. We may not understand them. Perhaps they do not benefit us, but — as you have already pointed out — we do as the others do so that the company can continue to function at its highest capacity. What happens at other companies when the profits fall, even slightly?"

Now Small, G., was beginning to sink. She could see it in his forehead, furrows that he likely didn't know were there.

"If there are enough complaints against you, I will have to address the problem. If your behaviour begins to impact the work of our other employees, mistakes will likely be made. Attention to detail will be lost. Sales will be affected. If we have to downsize, believe me, those with complaint folders this thick" — she held it up, feeling the power return to her side of the mahogany desk — "will be the first on the chopping block. Tell me, if you're worried now about where you should go, how will you feel then?"

Rapid blinking.

"Also, once you have been dismissed from Heaven, and so quickly after you started, you will not likely be hired by any of our sister companies. We simply will not be able to recommend you." In case there was any doubt in his mind, she rattled off the names of the attached bra and underwear company, the printing plant and shoe outlet store nearby, the organic grocery delivery that serviced nearly all of Heaven's staff, the popular online book retailer where he was a recognized customer, and fifteen additional companies — plus their subsidiaries — that she suspected Small, G., would find familiar, from the brand of muffins in the basement mall to the make of the faucets in the men's room.

"Also . . ." She touched the coffee mug, held that same finger forth as if begging him to focus on its hypnotic tip, and did not break her gaze. "I myself am under orders to report you if I believe your knowledge of the company's confidential *workings* may be a menace to the company at large. That kind of complaint does not just sit on my desk, nor on anyone else's desk in this building. It goes straight to Head Office, and it could mean your immediate termination. Tell me, does your knowledge of this company go beyond that of your co-workers?"

"No, ma'am."

He was placating her. She eyed him warily. "It is not a danger?"

"No, ma'am."

He was smart enough to placate her, she decided. That was what was happening. "I suggest you find your way to the parking garage at night, then." Lillian closed the folder. Beneath the desk, the feeling retreated — moved from her spine down the columns of her legs, curled up like her toes inside her shoes. Pleasant, she decided.

Small, G., employed an undersized voice to ask, "Are we done?" then glanced about the office as if both memorizing it and sussing out further ambushes.

Partly he reminded Lillian of a frightened rodent attempting to fight its way through a maze, his eyes scurrying across each surface for clues. Partly he reminded her of her younger self.

"There is one more thing." Lillian rose, approached her fax, retrieved the latest batch of pages, and shuffled through them. "Ah, here." She extended a faxed press clipping. The fuzzy ink read: CHLOE GOLD TO CHAMPION UNKNOWN AUTHOR." Small, G., reached for it, unsuspecting.

"Have you perhaps seen this already? It's been circulating around the building. My, but people do gossip," she said, facetiously. "If I recall correctly, Ms. Gold was your wife?"

"Yes —" Small, G., choked, and Lillian could see quite clearly that the word *wife* — or perhaps the content of the article itself — had sent a shameful colour rising in his cheeks.

She recalled that the name "Chloe Gold" had been Small's trump card during his initial interview, as if mere association were enough to grant him access to an entire industry.

"She isn't looking for *you*, is she, Gordon?"

Small's head jerked, but he kept his eyes downcast as if reading. He even held a finger aloft as if begging her to let him speak.

"I shouldn't think . . ." the man croaked without looking up. "We haven't spoken in almost eight years," he finished, meeting Lillian's gaze with eyes that looked more sad than scared. He wasn't a bad liar.

But he hadn't outright denied it. Lillian made a note. She wouldn't take it further — not just yet, she told herself, watching him creep to his feet. There were others to question. She opened the door for Small, G., and let the former suicide case head back to his little cage.

Alone again, she watched the LCD screen where his smudge stood mid-descent in the elevator. Aloud to herself, she said, "It's your job."

Without thinking, Lillian picked up the tepid mug and took a quick swallow of its contents, which were damp, bitter.

She slouched into her chair and ran her nails unconsciously through her hair, spiking it out above her forehead in a row of red thorns.

Near the back of the *Small, G.,* file was an envelope with "EVIDENCE — CONFIDENTIAL" stamped upon it. She shook it out and unsealed the tab, which had been opened and closed several times.

The note was typed on a single sheet of white letter paper, the thin sort, that must have been, Lillian guessed, torn from a typing tablet. There was no signature. Clearly Small, G., had had, while living, a romantic attachment to the typewriter and had eschewed the technology he now used daily at his job. At the same time, the letters punched into the typing paper were dry, barely there — a sign of the infrequency of his use of the ribbon that had borne witness to his last words. The words were not desperate so much as tired. They huffed across the page like breaths coming from someone who was winded, who had run or walked a long distance. They were not grand words, intelligent words, or even overly passionate. *Resigned*, Lillian thought. The feeling crept back up from her toes into her belly, seemed to push its head upward against her diaphragm, and she felt a sharp pang, like heartburn — or was it sadness, pity?

Lillian handled the file gently. She recognized the tenderness with which her fingertips traced the anorexic page. She had just put him through the wringer yet she found herself defending him in her mind. She closed her eyes. *You like him*, she accused herself, and found she couldn't deny it. *Why take the risk?*

"We are all security risks. When was the last time you asked yourself what you really get out of being mid-level management?"

The voice inside Lillian enthused with effervescent sarcasm, *Why, I ask myself that every morning! How did you guess?* Terminate him or promote him — Lillian knew those were the only two options for the disgruntled employee. Lillian reminded herself that Bentley, T., who had been a troublesome co-worker of hers at one point, had been content to preside over a foyer in a promotion that was little more than a title change.

"We can't promote him. That's not going to keep him quiet. He's already figured out that money doesn't matter. Even his most basic antics demonstrate that he has started to care about his co-workers, though — what they think, what they know. It's a backwards method of engaging with his community. We can use that." Quite suddenly Lillian opened her eyes. She picked up the pencil and tapped it against her teeth, enjoying the small shock she still got from the metal band against the enamel. "We can use that," she repeated.

The feeling inside her was still cocking its head. *That's why you think he should be spared if possible — he's a suicidal sap with a too-big heart.*

Lillian swirled around in her chair.

You're a sucker for cogs. Cog-sucker.

"Watch your language," Lillian warned herself aloud, even though she hadn't actually uttered the phrase.

20

GORDON LET OUT A SLUGGISH throat noise of detonation. Daves looked up from the onscreen page-spread he had been tweaking and highlighting with the cursor. Gordon slapped the door frame twice. Daves wheeled back, stood, and followed Gordon out of the office. Neither of them said a word until they had entered their private outdoor smoking cubicle. Then Gordon unfurled the faxed article from his pocket, the sticky note he'd previously affixed to his computer screen now hanging off the paper's edge.

"Got a rider there." Daves put his hand out and caught the neon note before it could fall into the snow. "Lillian Payne's phone number? She liked our stunt, then?" He grinned as he handed back the sticky, but the comment was pure nerves.

"It's my ex's number. I attached it to my workstation in case of emergency."

"What — When HR requested you to go up? Thought you weren't coming back?" The scoff was semi-serious. A crease had appeared on Daves' forehead.

Gordon nodded. "Never know."

"That should be your motto." Daves extended an open hand for the fax sheet. "C'mon."

Gordon unfolded the page and read aloud. Between the morning's encounter with Chandler and his ride down from Lillian's office, he had the words nearly memorized.

"W-T-F?" Daves pronounced each letter, invoking an expression Gordon knew well from his time at Whoopsy's, but which, like all Daves' favourites, was several years out of date. Daves' hands shook as he pulled out the package with three cigarettes. After watching Daves fumble with the foil, Gordon snatched it from him and mouth-retrieved one straight from the pack. Daves passed him a light, then seized the sheet and scanned the article.

"Keep it," Gordon muttered. "I have another copy back at my desk. That thing is breeding like a romance heroine."

Gordon watched as Daves' face drained.

Daves tapped the page and said, "Corporate mindset . . . If HR gives it to you, it's a warning. Big-time. Clear as a bell."

Gordon flicked the cigarette. Its droppings hit the crust of snow and rolled across it, gradually dispersing into black flakes.

"Scared?" Daves stammered around his own cigarette. "Cuz I wouldn't blame you if you were. But then there's proof. That's on our side, isn't it? I mean, if your ex-wife can't tell who it's by, who *is* going to know?"

"I'm not sure Chloe doesn't know. 'Flabbergasted.'" Gordon air-quoted. "The word implies some disbelief. My wife, my ex-wife, is the seeking type. Holding a massive search is just her style — drawing others into the drama — but it doesn't mean she's entirely in the dark." Even as Gordon said the words he felt himself reaching for his chest. He tapped the spot beside his heart, and ash from the cigarette tumbled down the front of his white shirt. Unbelievably, Chloe had read his book; he'd made contact. Strangely, he felt numb. But perhaps it was the cold air of the courtyard.

An actual expletive fell from Daves' mouth. "Then we're done. We're —"

The expletive fell again.

Although Gordon had used the word himself that very morning, he had heard it so few times during his months at Heaven that it now sounded like an absolutely foreign word.

"I can't afford this. There's — there's only one other job on my resumé," Daves sputtered. He dropped his cigarette in the snow and clutched at his collar with one hand. He bucked, his mouth making a gasping motion, though there wasn't any wheeze to accompany it.

"You're not having an asthma attack, Daves," Gordon assured him. One of Daves' hands remained pressed against his plaid shirt while the other reached out to Gordon's sleeve, clawing. Gordon shook it off like a minor irritant and circled the courtyard, pacing.

"I can't . . . I can't believe she read it," he said to himself. His steps turned to leaps.

Daves' hands dropped to his sides. He straightened. He scrunched his lips into an exaggerated scowl and, as Gordon came back around to his side, followed Gordon's gaze upward.

"My luck. My sheer, absolute, unadulterated luck, Daves." Gordon clasped him across the shoulders like a brother, a small smile hanging from his lips in spite of his friend's despondency. "And you, Daves, you made it happen."

Daves swore a third time — a string of profanity released in a gush. "Shit! Damn! Bastard! Motherfucking asshole!" The words trembled as they hung in the cold, still air in the court-yard in the centre of Heaven.

21

OVER THE YEARS LILLIAN had hired more than the 10,774 employees who currently served the building at 12205 Millcreek Industry Park occupied by Heaven Books, but there had been economic shifts, layoffs, promotions, demotions, and transfers. Although Heaven had its security systems to protect the workers from one another and to protect the company from any bold or blatant sabotage, it was simply not possible for Lillian to monitor the working habits of all ten thousand, seven hundred, seventy-four employees. The very idea twisted something in Lillian's spine and made her stand less straight.

Certainly individual e-mails could be accessed, and the number of outside calls made in a given week could be assessed to determine whether an employee's overly frequent attempts to contact a family member would threaten the company. But even then there were exceptional circumstances that were harmless when left alone. For instance, employee #1202, a Ms. Bitz, telephoned out every day at least once, but occasionally twice or even three times. Early on in the employment of #1202, the conversations had given rise to concern. Number 1202, Bitz, G., had a tendency to cradle the receiver for at least thirty minutes per day, conversing with a dial tone while believing contact was being made with the outside. It was a common habit, but thirty minutes was eight minutes higher than the company average. Reports had come back from Head Office asking Lillian to check into the situation.

In what was economically a colossal time-suck, as far as Lillian was concerned, her top IT person was contacted and given directives. The phone line of Bitz, G., was spliced and bugged, and Lillian Payne herself had to set aside time to go through the annoyingly one-sided conversations, transcribe them, and forward the transcriptions to Head Office along with her assessment of Bitz's psychological stability. It had made her feel like a petty department-store dick rather than an executive in a thriving company. Once the transcriptions had been received, Head Office assigned one of their own staff to reassess the conversations and confirm Lillian's findings. Verdict: harmless. In her branch alone, Lillian had calculated, $4,060 in salaried hours had been wasted investigating an excitable doting single mother. While Lillian understood the need to spend preventive and protective dollars, she weighed the gossip factor against them every time.

If yesterday's prime suspect had taken her advice and proceeded to the parking garage at the end of the workday, everything would have been a thousand times simpler. Instead, for whatever reason, the monitor showed him sitting at his desk again. This time, rather than tapping tirelessly at his keyboard, he had spent the night tapping a familiar thumb-sized plastic case, a pillbox that he had a tendency to treat as a rattle. Over and over he turned the box. At one point he had fed himself one of the small white antidepressants it contained. For the rest of the time he peered intently at it, unblinking, as if waiting for the exact moment the pill might reappear.

Today a long nail tapped the four hearts of Heaven — empty for the time being — and Lillian sat contemplating the risk factor of #1299, one Small, G., against the risk of rumour mongering from IT employee #8050 and how those rumours might affect the entire IT division, particularly — Lillian pursed her lips — employees #8036, #8039, and #8048. All of them were too questioning already, too restless, too dissatisfied, and too tactical. She knew they were looking for reasons — and methods — to unionize. Lillian placed a thin hand across her abdomen, the feeling — fear this time — rearing its head beneath her appendix. Unionization would shut the branch down immediately. Small, G., was small potatoes in comparison to that. Shorter hours, longer breaks, vacation time. With these demands achieved, she would have not one wanderer on her hands but ten thousand. The employees would realize that they deserved lives beyond what occurred at their desks.

Lillian worked her fingers around her hip and began adroitly massaging the muscles there. Heaven Corp. technology was out of date — and if she had told Head Office once she had told them a hundred times that she needed better!

"They work on beasts of computers," she said aloud to no one. Then she turned, catching her hand in mid-massage. She took the offending hand away, glaring at it.

She turned back toward her LCD screen and its closet — it had been recently installed, but even the surveillance system had been bought at a discount and couldn't zoom in for close-ups. She decided simply that the fruits of Small, G.'s labours between the hours of six in the evening and eight in the morning were likely not leaving the building via virtual communication. Like Heaven itself, he was the slightly out-of-date type, and although surveillance records had shown him in the Internet Division, they had also shown him with alarming frequency in the mailroom. If there was incriminating evidence to be found on employee #1299, surely it was sitting in some obvious desktop folder on his machine. All that needed to be done, then, was to physically remove his computer without giving him a moment to empty its files, and without arousing curiousity in IT about why the computer was being seized.

Lillian picked up her receiver and informed IT employee #8050 that the following morning there would be four new top-of-the-line computers for Floor Twelve.

"Yes, Heaven has received funding to conduct a temporary test of a brand-new editing software," Lillian invented, a thin smile draping her gums. "I would like these computers installed specifically in cubicles 129 to 133." After placing the call, Lillian dialled one of her assistant's extensions.

"We're experiencing some motivational problems on Floor Twelve . . . Yes, exactly, same old story," Lillian elaborated. "I need you to do some research today into editing software . . . Yes, I realize this isn't in your job description, but we're being creative," Lillian explained through gritted teeth.

She oughtn't to have explained herself at all. All she wanted was the hard drive.

"Just — just get the latest, whatever it is. Find it, pay for it, and have it ready for IT #8050 to install tomorrow morning . . . Yes, tomorrow, absolutely, regardless of cost. Order everything express. Also I need you to secure a copy of a specific Heaven title for me, one that just released this month, called *Deceptive Darling*. . . . No, first, get the software. Second, find the book. The software is priority. Well, yes, don't you *always* use my name on the purchase order?" Then, without thinking about it, Lillian blinked. Her eyes closed and popped open again, three times in rapid succession, in an expression of exasperation, though no one was there to see. She realized what she had done only afterwards. This flummoxed her further.

When Lillian laid a finger alongside her temple a moment later, she found that the corner of her eye was inexplicably wet. She pulled the digit away and examined it. A full droplet of water clung to the ovals of her fingerprint. *Impossible.* She flicked her finger and the globule fell onto the page before her. When it landed, it made a damp mauve blotch. *Small, G.,* was scrawled along the side of the folder where the drop had found its home. Lillian's hand darted forward jerkily, uncharacteristically, as if she had spotted a bug that needed killing. The tip of her index finger made contact with the tear that had recently left it, and when she pulled back again, her fingerprint remained, inked on the edge of Small's file. His name, indubitably lost.

IN WINDOW 12-I ON LILLIAN PAYNE'S LCD, employee #1299 stood above his new computer. The gear hunched. Lines of dust surrounded it, marking the shape occupied by its bulky predecessor. Manos, J., hurried into the window's edge, head swivelling, speaking above the cubicle walls so that all of the occupants could hear. Lillian crossed her arms, assessing, as the figures' lips moved silently. Two of the women on her monitor sat down, reached out, and turned on their new machines. The third began hastily cleaning up the dust lines with the help of a tissue. Only #1299, Small, G., remained standing, motionless.

"Has IT brought them up?" Lillian questioned the mouthpiece of her telephone. The reply was not the one she wanted to hear.

The camera that surveyed the cafeteria showed that #1202, Bitz, G., was still bingeing. She had been eating peanut butter and tuna-fish sandwiches interchangeably — always preparing them ahead and wrapping them in waxed paper, then retrieving them mere minutes later — stacks of them, for almost two weeks now. She no longer retired at the end of the day, just continued to order supplies from Eden Eats, placing the orders by telephone. Restaurant-size jars of mayonnaise. Paint buckets of Jif and generic jelly. It was an awful situation, one Lillian had not encountered before. Because no damage was being done — the exception being to Bitz's own bank account — Lillian had procrastinated on handling it. It was not priority, but it was gruesome. The short-term solution was to pull rank and get on the phone to Eden, have the employee's food service account suspended, but in the long term . . .

As she was waiting for her assistant to check in with IT and return her call with more positive news, Lillian felt a distinct acidic pang beneath her right ovary, as if a cyst had ruptured. She placed her hand over the spot and rapped the knuckles of her other hand repeatedly against the desk, harder and harder, to absorb the pain she felt inside. It was the fear again.

"Relax," she instructed herself, and attempted to straighten from her doubled-over stance. Eventually she was able to. Tentatively she shuffled a few steps around the outside of her office, one hand out to steady herself. Her palm trailed against the titles that packed her bookshelves tight. *Too Good to Be True, Careful What You Wish For, Kansas Casanova, Kiss TV, Miss Jitters and the Wedding Blues, Two Worlds: One Woman, Four-Alarm Man, Inspector Delectable, The PI's Private Side, Inspector Steele-Me-a-Kiss, The Sheik Can't Help It, Tough Tingles, The Nanny Assignment, Little Miss Yes, Naughty or Nice, Erogenous Zone #10, A Little Too Thirty for Love, Making Love in Manhattan, Make Love Not Murder, His vs. Hers, What a Girl Almost Wants, Brand New Heart, Designer Baby, The Splurging Virgin, The Wedding Impulse, New Year's Ever After, Husband on Call, Prime Suspect: Love, The Commitment-phobe, Affection Prone, Terminally in Love, Lovesick, Intensive Care, Diagnosis: Diamond.* Each shelf had its own shade, from candy floss to cantaloupe, raspberry to ruby red to watermelon, each series with a shelf to itself, an unending line of uniform design, and each so snug against its neighbour that Lillian felt no hesitation leaning upon them as if they composed a solid wall.

"I'm fine," she proclaimed, patting the spines of the books as if reassuring a set of old friends. "Just fine." She squared her shoulders and let her hand drop from her belly. Inside her garnet jacket pocket was a compact. Lillian removed it and with quivering fingers snapped it open, held it to reflect her pale, pointed face. She located a tube of lipstick and reddened her lips. "All right." She snapped the compact tight and dropped the personal items back into her pocket. Her hands smoothed down the front of her outfit. She stood tall and shook her head. "All right," she began to say again, but the sound came out as a growl. With a single jab of that phantom pain, she felt her backside slide down the ridge of each shelf until she came into contact with her office carpeting. As she dropped she pulled a reddish surf of Heaven titles down with her.

It took a few minutes before she regained her composure. She massaged herself with both hands, and then, feeling assured the pain had passed and spying the glistening red and pink chaos around her, Lillian did something that was very uncommon to her. At first she did not process what it was, it had been so long since she had heard the sound or made the shape that produced it. When she finally did, she nodded her head ever so slightly and made it again, recognizing the revving noise as a laugh. She reached out and heartily slapped one of the paperbacks with her palm so that it made a satisfying *smack*. She picked up the title and thwacked the pile with it repeatedly.

When she stopped, *Darling Deception* was dangling from two fingertips above her creased lap.

"That *girl* —" she sputtered.

"That *assistant* —" she corrected herself.

Black flats smashed cover corners as Lillian regained her feet quickly and tramped across her own archive of titles. She reached her desk. She laid the bristling book upon it. The fear inside her had accumulated again, into a tight knot in the kidney area on the left side. She covered it with one quivering palm. Her other hand jerked the receiver to her ear. She had reached out to dial her assistant when she realized there was no dial tone. "Hello? Hello . . . Lillian Payne here."

Lillian cocked her head and the assistant's voice crept into her ear. "Oh, it's you. Didn't I ask you to locate a copy of *Darling Deception* for me?" Lillian barked. "I've had to do it myself."

Lillian paused.

"I did?" she queried the receiver, her shoulders falling, her palm creeping around to her back again. "Yes, yes, I suppose I did say the new software was top priority. . . . You were calling me? Head Office? On line two?" Lillian listened to her voice rise in pitch with each question, and watched her right hand shake as her finger plunged toward the lit button on the telephone.

The sentences that tumbled out of Lillian Payne's mouth sounded to her professional ears like those of a nervous intern. "Of course, of course. I have the folders on my desk. I haven't interviewed them all, but as many as I could possibly get through in one day. Warnings have been issued, and — We will soon —

"Yes, I have read the book," Lillian lied, clamping her lips tightly together after the words had left them.

At that moment the door to her office was flung forcibly open, knocking against the door jamb as a ponytailed IT man, #8050, began unloading computers from a long dolly. Behind him the apologetic face of Lillian's assistant bobbed.

"I've begun a search —" Lillian covered the telephone receiver and mouthed, *Leave them*. Her shooing failed.

Number 8050 tapped the dolly, his ring finger knocking against it with a *tink, tink* of gold band on metal. He had no intention of leaving the whole cart; he wanted the dolly. Lillian put a finger to her lips and he began swinging towers and monitors onto the carpet. The machinery rattled, stray plastic mice and keyboards skittered — unloaded less gently, they twisted on their cords and fell, clattering. The dolly screeched as it exited, particularly as it made the drop from Lillian's plush carpet into the reception area.

"Yes," she said with firmness, attempting to inject into the single word the calm of any ordinary task, the simplicity of tomato selecting in a grocery. "Yes. The background noise you hear is the arrival of the computers. Some of the suspects. My assistant is just setting them up now."

The wide-eyed assistant skulked from the doorway warily, as if by simply entering the office she might become culpable in whatever discussion was occurring. With adolescent gawkiness the girl eyed the computers but did not bend to move any of them or begin plug sorting.

Lillian's hand revolved, an imaginary kite-string collector. *Hurry.* "Yes," she said again. "Absolutely. I agree that the incident has reached the stage where we must take action. I'd only been waiting for word from you. I haven't the slightest idea how this could have occurred, but if it did originate from someone specific within our branch — and the key word there, I think, is *if* —"

A hard-drive tower plunked upon Lillian's desk. The assistant disappeared beneath the desk in search of a socket.

"I understand the risks to profits and to the company at large . . ." Lillian cleared her throat and straightened her shoulders, feeling her sense of power return once again.

Her own terminal went dead.

"There is no way we will allow the author to contact Chloe Gold, her agent, or . . ."

A power cord untangled.

". . . any other publishing agent."

The drive of Small, G., began to boot across the face of Lillian's monitor.

"I understand how damaging a romance that ends in suicide could be for our reputation as a company, particularly now that it has hit the public consciousness and gained such notoriety — and I as much as anyone had hoped it would not. As far as the situation at this branch is concerned, I —"

*Username: gsmall. Password: ******

"I am in complete control."

One hand spread across her throat and collarbone as Lillian eased down into her chair and clicked the hard-drive icon. She opened the folder labelled *My Docs,* where she discovered an open-mouthed hole of a headline: *0 files.*

22

ACROSS THE CUBICLES Gordon's co-workers were singing the refrain of Chloe Gold. With each use the name's currency seemed to diminish, for *Chloe Gold* had become — seeing as Gordon had no name, was simply *unknown* — a substitute for Gordon's own. It was January fifth, and Heaven was ringing in the New Year with gossip, passed from station to station via e-mail and swift whisper. Ivy Wolfe from the Internet Division had already forwarded Gordon 251 Google Alerts pertaining to the scandal.

Did you hear? It originated in our branch. . . . Over the holidays! Already three members of the sales force have been terminated. . . . I heard it was five. . . . They're conducting a company-wide search. . . . We're all under review. . . . Have you read it? . . . I read it. I didn't think much of it . . . I just started. . . . I'm reading it now. . . . It's good. It's gorgeous. It's glorious, godly, gothic, gives me goose pimples. . . . Are you kidding? We don't need that guff, it's a gaffe! . . . Can't knock Gold, though, good God.

Amid the gushing hysteria Gordon dropped a petunia petal of an envelope into the outbox beside Bentley's podium, which was still draped with tinsel. Beneath the miniature sketchy *To* he'd printed the name *C. Small* on the envelope.

"Something for Mom?" Bentley queried. "Using company postage?"

"A bit belated." It was the truth.

Bentley eyed him sternly, tsked and tutted, but that was all.

Gordon watched as James Ames arrived, slung the outbox over his shoulder, and with typical slackness didn't bother collecting from Design that day. Ames hoisted the mail into the elevator, where he set the box down on top of his cart without emptying it. The doors slid shut and Gordon turned to Bentley and nodded before he wound his way back through the cubicles. Gordon imagined the box riding down to the basement, his pink no. 2 envelope lying on top, the first paragraph showing through its underside in the bunched lines of his childlike penmanship before the fold of the Heaven stationery obscured the rest from view:

Dear Chloe,

I know you will recognize this as my handwriting. I cannot tell you how I managed to reach you, but please believe what I have to tell you. At one point I blamed you for the disintegration of our marriage, but after writing our story, I cannot. You are the beneficiary of my very limited estate, and there is one thing of value I bequeathed to you, which may now come in handy — my literary rights. . . .

23

LILLIAN'S FEET FOUND THEIR WAY around her office without assistance from her eyes. She twisted her door handle and greeted the figure on her threshold with a raised hand but did not raise her lids. A purplish paperback was making its way around the office in front of her face. She nimbly avoided the bank of misplaced, disconnected computers, and parked herself and the open book behind her desk even as she licked her index finger and turned to the next page. "Listen to this," she said. "'We could have been the same person, given the level of hatred that existed between us, if only it hadn't been one-sided. It was that alone, I think, that defined us as two.' Isn't that profound?"

"Cliché, I thought," Small, G., replied. "Bitter treacle. But what do I know?"

It was only then that Lillian looked up from *Darling Deception* and saw who stood before her. She nodded vaguely and flipped another page.

"You called me up?" came his impertinent voice.

Lillian closed the lavender love story and placed it on the desk in front of her. "Yes."

She looked down at the single page on her desk: the smeared photocopy that had been faxed to department heads, then recirculated. The man in the green suit let his gaze fall upon it as well.

Lillian reached across the desk and shuttled the page to his side. "I've never seen what all the fuss was about, personally. . . ."

Small, G., arched his eyebrows.

"With Chloe Gold," she added.

"I don't know. Perhaps she is better than I previously gave her credit for," the green-suited slump offered.

"Oh, but you would say that — *now*," Lillian spat. Small, G., was too smug for his own good. It brought the pain back, rising in her esophagus, especially when she thought of the pleasure she had been receiving mere minutes earlier, reading his gilt-covered concoction. "The problem is that your novel has burst out and is running loose out there in the world." She laughed, but even to her ears it was a cold, sober laugh. There it was. She had acknowledged him as the author, explicitly, without innuendo. *Darling Deception* lay on the dustless surface between them. "You don't know what it's done to me, Gordon."

His stuttering self took over, and Lillian knew that her casual use of his name was part of the reason why. "I — I thought you liked it. Just a minute ago —"

"Don't be so self-conscious. I do. I love it. I adore it. I am your devoted fan." She closed her eyes. When she opened them again, she said, "But it's caused a shit storm. That's right, you heard me — a shit storm. I can say that now. I've got Dave

David down in Production cursing full hurricanes these days, words and combinations we haven't heard in Heaven since the '60s. Complaints are coming in faster than you can type —" In case he doubted her, she snatched a dictionary-thick file from the drawer and held it high.

Hefting up another folder in her other hand, she added, "Of course, there's also some fan mail for our 'author,' Allison Sharpe. But do you know how much we've had to pay out to the *real* Allison Sharpe? She'll be 'Gwendolyn Small' henceforth. But the woman wasn't happy, and her new contract is costing Heaven a pretty penny."

Lillian plunged on without pause. "We've got reports from Head Office that Chloe Gold has been attempting to contact you via a medium. Yes, a $300-per-hour psychic. Contrary to what you might think, we *do* monitor attempts at incoming messages. You never know when one might break through. Apparently you're in a 'better place' now," she harrumphed.

"And Georgianne Bitz has ceased going to her car at night or even making a pretense at work." Lillian snatched at a stack of messages that sat impaled on a spike beside the telephone. Without disengaging the papers from their murderer, she waved the contraption in Small, G.'s face like a fencer. "Nearly everyone you've come into contact with is beginning to doubt our entire system. Editorial is in complete upheaval. Do you know what that does to me? You won't believe this, but I am feeling physical pain. I know, it's not possible. It's hysterical. It's utterly illogical. But suddenly I am feeling in *every fibre of my being* —"

She waved her hand frantically. "Stupid phrase, culled from decades of working here, strike that, nix, delete —" With her arm Lillian looped an editor's symbol in the air, an invisible diagonal line with a pig's tail. "However, you must understand that you, Mr. Small, have started something unheard of. You've set us all on a destructive path. A path of indecision. We're becoming un-Heavenly, do you understand?"

Small, G., blinked. The green worm. How could he just sit there blinking?

Lillian thrust her face directly into his and blinked back at him, an exaggerated mockery of his action. "It's not even about us. So we can feel. *Whatever!*" Lillian stalked around her office. "It's about business. If books with unhappy endings start to sell — Holy fudge," she said out of habit. "We'll be out of jobs. Do you know where we'll go if we wind up out of work?"

Small, G., shook his head.

"Neither do I. But that's exactly what we're up against. In less than one week's time, your book, your little *Darling*" — she seized it, waved it in the air, and flung it down in front of him — "has become a buzz book. Now, that's not to say that it's good, although . . ." she amended, grabbing her copy and swiftly finding a folded corner. She displayed the page for Small, G., to see. ". . . I do rather envy this passage. But" — the fondness fell from her voice — "regardless of its merits, it has picked up incredible steam in terms of its sales and the discussions it is creating. This is horribly embarrassing for the company. Nothing like this has ever happened. I mean, there have been minor revolts, a pulled fire alarm now and again, the occasional haunting, problem cases, transfers, talk of unions, but this . . . this is public. Thankfully I'm in HR, not PR. As you can imagine, down there on Sixty-Seven they are scrambling right now, absolutely scrambling to come up with explanations that will please the press. It's a scandal book. It will make millions, Gord," she concluded abruptly. She found to her surprise that the faster she talked, the more she could feel. Tears were streaking her cheeks.

"So . . . you're on my side?" he squeaked hopefully.

Lillian circled the desk. She could feel flames practically leaping from her fingers as she rapped them upon the wood, and from her eyes as she assessed him. "I'm most certainly *not*, as you put it, 'on your side.' Have you got a rubber-band ball for a brain? Autograph this —" she commanded him, thrusting her copy of *Darling Deception* into his hands and providing him a purple felt-tip pen. "We thought, we expected, when it first came to our attention, that this title would be an embarrassment, that it would ruin our reputation with romantics the world over, that it would bring the company down a notch — more than a notch. But it's a cruel, cruel thing, Mr. Small. It's just the opposite. There are reviews. A popular author gets behind it. It's touted as a discovery. Suddenly its faults, the things that would normally go against it, such as its melancholic nature, its self-conscious format, become *desirable*. If this book is a success — and it already is — it puts all of us in peril. The market is now open to other books like it, and if we don't produce them, one of our competitors will. In 1955 our readers wanted front-porch romances tied up in apron strings, with only the odd allusion to the bedroom. Now, apparently, they want apocalypse in their love stories: qu-queer content," she stuttered, "irreconcilable differences, divorce, depression, stalking, SSRIS.

"If I don't report you to Head Office, immediately, as the author of this volume" — Lillian slapped shut the cover of the copy Small had guiltily signed — "this branch will be shut down and we will all be cast into an unemployable void. All of us, your precious Chandler Goods, Georgianne Bitz, Dave David, Ivy Wolfe, Erika Workman, Jill Fast, Fleur Janisse, Titus Bentley, Jonathan Manos — employees 1 through 10,775, *me*, *you*. So I am not on your side. I am simply here, trying to hold all the ends together."

"So do you —"

Lillian didn't look up from her face-cupped hands.

"Do you still like my novel?"

"Please . . ." Lillian answered in a voice she had not heard herself use in decades, one she recognized as meek. She brushed her hair back from her face with her fingers. "I can't love it." She reeled Gordon's renegade paperback into her lap with a covetousness that she had never expected to feel. "Not when I absolutely hate you right now. Listen to me, I sound positively seven years old, tossing about words like *hate*. You'd never guess how old I really am. I suppose, under stress, we are all susceptible —"

"What happens?" Small, G., interrupted her.

"Hmm?"

"If you don't report me?"

"I have your signed confession," Lillian stated. With a crisp nod she indicated the autographed copy of *Darling Deception*. "'Gordon Small,'" she read from the title page. "Gordon Small, not Allison Sharpe, has signed my copy."

"But — but —" Small, G., said. He was stunned, she could see, that even during her outpouring of emotion she had managed to trick him. "What if you don't?" he finally managed.

"But why wouldn't I?"

Their eyes met and held.

"There may be things I don't understand," the man said softly, "about Heaven, about how the company works, or how it derives profits from —" He waved his hand in front of his face as if something smelled. "Or why profit should even matter at this point. But what if there's another chance for me?"

When Lillian spoke next, she could feel her office growing smaller, more claustrophobic, the thousand lines in a thousand romance books coming to life from the shelves to pull piano wire around her throat. "You would plunge all of us into *nothingness* for that chance at success? Fame? *Glory?*" She knew that the way she said the words made them sound dirty, uncouth.

The olive-suited man looked up helplessly. "I'm afraid . . ." He cleared his throat in a stalling manner. ". . . I have already."

Lillian stood up, turned around, her back to him. She braced herself. "You mean this?" When she faced him, the envelope fell, unopened, softly as she had intended, petal-like from her sleeve. *C. Small.*

Small, G., received the envelope. He tipped it up on one corner and spun it round, examined it as intently as a man signing a contract. They both looked at it: invitation-sized, unblemished, and most important, without postmark. Small, G., let it drop, placed a palm over his eyes, and ran the hand down his entire face. "Ames?" he snapped, but it was less a question than an acknowledgement of defeat.

"Mr. Ames is now making fifty cents more per hour. You can't hold it against him. He's just an essence, after all, who has been coerced into believing he has form. He's still susceptible to greed, as are most of us. Heaven Corporation is a business. We exploit an opportunity and provide a valuable service in return. Without our guidance, most souls wander. They crave routine, regulation, a system of rewards, socialization. We can provide that. And in exchange, we get a workforce. It's not as if we don't offer choice. We own an astounding number of businesses in different fields — from manufacturing to media — and our temp agencies are adept at placing post-body beings in any type of workplace that may be desired. Happy souls, for the most part. And they drive a booming economy!"

"But . . . ?"

"As long as there have been people, there have been entrepreneurs. Wherever a profit can be made, why not make it? Heaven and your co-workers are one and the same. They're happy here, Gordon, even if you haven't been."

Lillian gently put out her hand and touched his sleeve. "You have a choice, Gordon," she said.

24

FOR THE FIRST TIME EVER, Gordon had been promoted. A position had been created especially for him. He would have his own office. He would have his own window. He would have his own horizontal blinds. He did not yet know whether he would look out over an embankment, a concrete cul-de-sac, or a shimmering night sea of skyscraper windows. All he knew was what he had been told. GORDON SMALL had been stencilled on the door of a room in Heaven's head office, and it was there he would spend eight hours a day, five days a week rewriting *Darling Deception* to fit different characters into different settings. He would toil under the names Allison Sharpe, Laurie Little, and Andi Moore-Smith, along with any others that Heaven saw fit to assign him. Essentially he would rewrite the story of his relationship with Chloe Gold to suit the desires of the masses. One day Chloe would be blond, the next, brunette. One day Gordon would be Graham, the next day, Grant. First he would kill himself by hanging, then throw himself before a subway car. One day she would have another lover, and the next day ten — women, men, the specifics were changeable. He would be envisioning a dozen Chloes each month for eternity.

Gordon very much wished to find himself beneath a subway car at this moment.

"Initial here, here, here." An uncapped pink pen accompanied the swift appearance of Gordon's new contract. Lillian pointed at self-evident intervals down the page. "A representative from Head Office will be coming immediately to collect you to complete the transfer. It would be best to have this signed for his arrival."

Gordon squinted at the words.

"You understand that the company is hiring you to create stories that are identical in tone to *Darling Deception*, that follow the same plot formula but utilize new and exciting characters, each with their own particular foibles. Each story should be different from its predecessor, yet the reader should leave each book with the exact same feeling. You understand that you shall write such content for no other company besides Heaven Books. You understand that this is a salaried position and hence your royalty rate is reduced, and that you are not entitled to any additional monies from foreign sales. You understand that at present you are under contract for one hundred such titles, and that you are obligated to produce them to the deadlines Heaven sets."

Gordon's hand quivered and the pen fell.

Lillian reached out and took his fingers in hers. She grasped them and squeezed. Her skin felt warmer than he remembered from the handshake after their first interview, and he realized it was the first time they had touched without a static shock. "Have you said goodbye to Georgianne Bitz yet?"

Gordon nodded.

"Heaven's career counsellors are top-notch. She's really doing better, isn't she?"

Gordon nodded.

"And Dave David?"

A third time he nodded.

Lillian picked up the pen and handed it to him.

His signature looked strange as it peered up at him, swimming. "I feel sick to my stomach," Gordon croaked.

"It's only a feeling. You'll get over it." Lillian stood and whisked the papers out of his sight. "William — Bill, is it?" she bandied cheerily over Gordon's shoulder. He saw that the door had opened. A pot-bellied bald man in a silver suit and too-pointy shoes filled its frame.

"Sure is." The man came at them with his hand out. They seized it in succession, first Lillian, then Gord, and pumped. Gordon had the distinct impression that this Bill and Lillian Payne had never met, hence the crackling grins of overcompensation. "Lillian," Bill said as salutation, and Lillian was suddenly luminous. Gordon watched her hover around the room.

"Gordie. Mind if I call you that?" Bill directed the question at him in a way that left no room for quibbling. A backslap came out of the handshake.

"Are you my boss?" Gordon wondered aloud, warily.

Bill exploded. "Me?! Oh no, I'm just a representative of the company."

"We have the paperwork all ready, Bill, and Mr. Small's desk is being packed up as we speak, so unless I can get you a coffee, I think we're all set." The three of them stood nodding as if their heads had metal cranks that had been wound by unseen hands. "Well then, I'll escort you down."

On Floor Twelve the three of them collected Gordon's things. Bentley was waiting when the elevator doors opened. He held out an oversized cardboard box that contained Gordon's sole literary publication aside from *Darling Deception*, a snow globe that had haunted his cubicle since his arrival but did not actually belong to him, his Georgianne Bitz–graced Sunlight mug, a half-box of tea bags, a Visine bottle, and one reprimand from Chandler Goods. As the box left his hands and fell into Gordon's, Bentley snarl-smiled as if he had never taken Gordon into his confidence.

"Well, that'll do ya," Bill yodelled, clapping the box on the side.

Lillian rode down to the basement with them. She remained in the elevator as Gordon and Bill exited. Gordon turned and took in her commanding figure one last time, framed in the pristine light of the elevator. Her eyes creased at the corners as she shot him a chilling smile. "I'll be fine," she said, but he noticed her hand slip around to her spine to massage it just before the elevator doors closed out the light.

Bill had come by company car, and he explained to Gordon that he would be given one too. It had probably been delivered already and was likely sitting in the garage at Heaven Central that moment. "But for now you'd better ride with me, son. Head Office can be a little hard to find," Bill said out of the side of his mouth as they walked briskly across the parking complex to the visitors' section.

"Everyone is looking forward to meeting you," Bill went on. His hand nestled between Gordon's neck and shoulder, clapping and nudging constantly. Bill's fingers felt like talons. The big man pressed on. "Can't wait to see what you got for us. Heard your cynicism is number one. Where'd you get your ideas anyway? They say it's best to write from your life experience. You write from your life experience? If so, you're going to be writing your life like *Track One: Repeat*, cuz we want you with us for a *long*, long time. You're going to make such a name for yourself." Bill hooted. "Well, three, actually — Allison, Laurie, and Andi."

"There it is —" Bill gestured toward a lustrous distant Infiniti, extending his arm with the remote control to unlock the vehicle and automatically start it.

As soon as his hand left Gordon's shoulder, Gordon choked, "I quit," and bolted. The box fell and the miscellany scattered, snow globe and coffee cup shattering across Bill's polished shoes, ceramic and tiny plastic flecks. Gordon darted across the parking garage. It was a split-second decision. They couldn't cast out the occupants of Heaven, 12205 Millcreek Industry Park, if the one and only problem had removed itself. Gordon didn't know if this was another suicide attempt or if this time it was an actual sacrifice on his part. He only knew he couldn't go, couldn't let those dreadful books be born from him into the world. Already he could see them before his eyes: twins, triplets, sextuplets, multiples of one another.

Bill sputtered, "Gordon! Get back here! This is not part of my job. You don't know me when I'm PO'ed." The flat bottoms of dress shoes scraped cement, followed by the pounding of sneakers, and without looking back, Gordon knew that Security had joined the Head Office rep in the chase.

There was no way they could catch him, he reasoned; he could run forever. If their physicality really meant nothing, three grown men could chase one another at equal distances without gain, without ceasing. With no clear plan, Gordon headed automatically for the Z section of the garage, the alphabet signage flying past him from where it hung on the pillars. Like a kid he stuck out a finger, trailed it along the hoods of cars in Section F as he passed, leaving his imprint in their dust. As he sprinted, the image that sprang into his mind was not of Chloe Gold, although her kind eyes and bountiful lips were easy enough to recall — he passed by G, H, I, J — but of himself outside the bookstore, as if seen from above: a small man on the sidewalk, lingering, face mashed with jealousy that he no longer understood. The signs for K and L leapt past him. His legs blurred at such a clip that the muscles they were made of seemed to mesh with the lost spaces through which they passed. M, N, O, P plummeted away and Gordon came so swiftly to S it surprised him, made something in his stomach kick with sweet-sick determination. His shoes did not even seem to fight for traction. What happened after Heaven? He barely had time to ask. On he ran, and on, farther than he believed the parking garage could go.

He was long past Z when he felt his body dispersing like the letters. *This is how it must feel when a star shoots and burns out.*

A split-second later he realized that he was more like something re-entering Earth's atmosphere — he was hanging on that line between the dead and the living, and since he wasn't large enough or fast enough, the force of it would cause his disintegration. *Every fibre of my being,* he thought wildly, hilariously. Then the thought turned to air.

It became darker and darker, and as it did, Gordon felt himself fade, felt himself and his name fuse once and for all — happily — with obscurity.

ACKNOWLEDGEMENTS

Thanks to my publisher and editor, Lynn Henry, for shaping and making my strange little fantasy into this book. Thanks to Sarah MacLachlan, Julie Wilson, Ingrid Paulson, and everyone at House of Anansi. Thanks to Don Sedgwick and Shaun Bradley of the TransAtlantic Literary Agency. For continued faith and friendship, thanks to Michael Holmes. Thanks especially to my family and the Davis family for support, and to Brian, who inspires and incites.

An early passage from this novel appeared in *Taddle Creek* magazine. I am also grateful to the Canada Council, the Ontario Arts Council, and my grant recommenders for financial assistance.

ABOUT THE AUTHOR

 EMILY SCHULTZ is widely recognized as one of Canada's best young writers. She is the author of the acclaimed novel *Joyland* and the story collection *Black Coffee Night*, which was shortlisted for the ReLit Award and the Danuta Gleed Literary Award. She has also published a book of poetry, *Songs for the Dancing Chicken*, which was a finalist for the Trillium Book Award. Her writing has appeared in numerous publications, including the *Globe and Mail*, *The Walrus*, *Black Warrior Review*, and *Geist*, and in several anthologies. She lives in Toronto, where she teaches creative writing and edits Joyland.ca, which the CBC called "the go-to spot for readers seeking the best voices in short fiction."